LILLIPUTIN

SEAGULL
BOOKS
•
CELEBRATING
40 YEARS

THE CZECH LIST

Jan Němec

LILLIPUTIN

Tales from a War

Translated by
DAVID SHORT

LONDON NEW YORK CALCUTTA

MINISTRY OF CULTURE
CZECH REPUBLIC

This publication has been supported by
the Ministry of Culture of the Czech Republic

Seagull Books, 2023

First published in Czech as *Liliputin. Povídky z války* by Jan Němec

© Jan Němec, 2022

© Host – vydavatelství, s.r.o., 2022

First published in English translation by Seagull Books, 2023

English translation © David Short, 2023

ISBN   978 1 80309 301 7

British Library Cataloguing-in-Publication Data

A catalogue record for this book is available from the British Library

Typeset at Seagull Books, Calcutta, India

Printed and bound in the USA by Integrated Books International

For Oksana

Only the dead
are safe;
only the dead have seen
the end of war.

   —Santayana

Contents

Saboteur

He turned the ignition key. The cameras concealed about the car's body showed him his immediate surroundings via the screen on the dashboard. The red Alfa Romeo to the left belonged to the lady next door, whom he had once quite fancied, while the Škoda on the other side meant nothing. He reversed out of their embrace without triggering a single annoying bleep and stopped briefly in the middle of the street with his hands resting on the wheel. He glanced at the screen—it showed an aerial view of his car surrounded by smudgy yellow blotches where the wet roadway reflected the street lights. His mobile automatically paired with the speakers and up came the Rewrite History podcast on Spotify that he'd missed the end of last time. 'It's like on a par with Romania, it's not—' he switched it off from the steering wheel. Raindrops were trickling down the windscreen, which was supposed to start the wipers automatically, but the sensors were being dilatory. He turned the wipers on manually, took a deep breath, in, and out, put the car in gear and drove off up the familiar, oh-so-familiar street.

It was almost eleven-thirty. He'd thought it best to set out straightaway; if he'd left it till morning, he'd never have got away:

in the morning, you wake up, do your teeth and just get on with life. Even if you don't have one.

His hands on the wheel began to feel cold, so he put the heating on. He hadn't gone far before he passed the pub on the corner where the previous evening he'd met up with a girl he'd known at university. Some things need time before they can be judged in the round, while others never jell into a whole. The girl, who had been quite unapproachable at uni, asked him that evening if he was pleased to have achieved all the things he'd talked about ten years before, and for the fifth time in twenty minutes she ran her fingers through her hair. He was surprised that she remembered what he had talked about back then. And that she thought he'd achieved something. He had briefly wondered if sleeping together after a lapse of ten years made any sense but two beers later rejected the idea. He'd ordered a cab but then didn't take it.

Several crossroads later, each marked out by a single flashing amber light, he left the city behind. Gradually, fewer proper buildings, but more warehouse facilities. He passed them by as well and stopped at the first petrol station out in the wilds. What they'd said on the news was true, at least something of what they'd said on the news was verifiably true: during the last week, petrol had gone up by almost three crowns a litre. Not that that mattered, it still reeked the same however much it cost. He thrust the nozzle down the fuel-filler neck, hmm, this is about the limit to any violence I'm capable of, he thought. He looked about him with the vague realization that he quite liked petrol stations that were open at night. Islets amid a distant void, citadels of civilization. It's great when glass doors slide open before you in the middle of the night and you can treat yourself to coffee and a baguette and stare vacantly into the eyes of the person behind the counter.

'Number four, paying by card,' he paid for a full tank and five pre-packed baguettes. He hadn't had much in the house, and he hadn't wanted to waste time packing anything. Initially, he'd grabbed a suitcase to toss some clothes in, but then thought arriving with a tourist's suitcase full of underwear wasn't the greatest idea. So he'd taken just a sports bag from the closet and stuffed it with the first things that came into his head. It was obvious from the outset that he was taking all the wrong things, but he did pack some energy bars, thermal underwear and a sleeping bag.

He couldn't have said how he was feeling, but the car's display had a calming effect, so somewhere inside he must have been feeling nervous. The screen glimmered and when he turned on the satnav it was taken over by a cobweb of roads. He entered his destination, with GPS that's simple, geography is way easier terrain to survey than biography, and the map immediately highlighted several options. Via Poland, or Slovakia? By the more northerly route it would take three hours less, but he knew Slovakia from his travels there as a child with his parents, and that's the route he'd prefer. In the end he wasn't that bothered, it would all be the same at night, and by daybreak he'd be so muzzy that whether they were Polish fields or Slovak he was passing, Polish villages or Slovak, he simply wouldn't notice much.

He wove his way out of the petrol station and realized this might be his last chance to phone. Midnight, still okay. Zuzana goes to bed late, she's in the habit of writing when all's gone quiet and other people's thoughts don't come crawling over her lines. But if he did phone, he'd have to say something; that's the trouble with phones. He'd much rather just listen to her—if only she might read something to him the way he used to read to her when they were still living together, the way he would read to her when she was away on business and couldn't get to sleep in hotel rooms. But that was exactly what would call for some explaining and explanations were something he baulked at. He took out his phone and began flicking through his downloaded audiobooks, if only for the company of somebody's voice, but soon realized he'd got himself in a muddle again.

He moved up into top gear and switched to cruise control. His headlights dissolved the blocks of darkness and he sailed on inside his mobile capsule disturbed only now and again by another car. He gradually drifted into motorway mooning, a kind of slipshod hypnosis. Between Olomouc and Ostrava, he tried to piece together the names and surnames of all his classmates at primary school: Dana Hančikovská, Michal Chromý, Alena . . . what was it? Between Ostrava and Katowice, he tried to recall all the trainers he'd worn as a teenager. Sometime at around fifteen, he'd used the money from his first summer job to buy some Pumas, ring trainers they were, Puma brand.

He had his first sense of malaise somewhere between Katowice and Kraków, by which time he'd done nearly 400 kilometres. He knew Kraków, he couldn't deny how easy it would be to get a bed for the night, have a good night's sleep, and in the morning go and have breakfast in that coffee shop overlooking the Vistula. When you wake up in the morning, there's nothing to stop you simply getting on with life: somewhere between individuality and invalidity. Being oneself just isn't a problem. There's nothing more restricted than one's own identity, which is precisely why it gets given most support, but if others can manage it, why shouldn't he be able to? At the roundabout his head was in such disarray that he drove right round it twice, but eventually he did find the right exit for the E40 motorway.

His journey continued uneventful and untroubled by thoughts. Just once, in some small town or other, the lights turned red on him, a drunk set off to cross the road and goodness knows what made him toot his horn at him. This scared the man, who turned towards the car and waved his arms in an odd way, something between surprise and menace. He flashed his lights at him, the drunk shaded his eyes and tried to peer inside the car. He probably thought someone he knew was trying to attract his attention; but who knows me? the driver thought.

*

Day was breaking. The horizon first donned a sample of light, but half an hour later the sun was lolling about on the horizon directly ahead of him. He realized that you don't have to have slept and morning will still mean something. Inside the human eye, there are cells that have nothing to do with seeing but are light-sensitive and trigger biological rhythms accordingly. He closed his eyes and slowly counted to ten. Knowing of course that just as a man's cells don't bother him with questions, his car's accident-prevention systems wouldn't let him crash. Nature and motor-vehicle manufacturers are agreed that living is a good thing. Hard to argue with that. Nonetheless he believed that people underestimated the losses brought about by birth.

Road signs were carrying increasing numbers of UA codes. U-A U-AAA he launched the interjections into the silence of the car's interior and waited to see if anything would happen.

The queue at the frontier shouldn't be too long from this side. He noticed that most cars were parked up on the hard shoulder with their engines off, waiting for people from the other side. A number of repurposed shipping containers and stalls stood on a concreted open space and just then two women happened to be carrying a huge tea urn across to one of them. Briefly he hesitated, he could park up, have a cup of tea and ask how things were looking, and he might even try the internet.

He'd last seen the news the evening before. The couple who'd got married in a city under siege and had their wedding photos taken wearing camouflage and holding automatic rifles. The woman who'd given birth to twins in the metro and was as happy as if she were in some clinic in Switzerland. And again he saw that old man who had knelt down in front of a tank.

It all left a nasty taste in his mouth. The news should really be about the latest draft legislation and inflation, so as to leave no one in doubt that the day's main events are utterly meaningless. He found it unbearable when his colleagues at the law firm adorned their profile pictures with a Ukrainian flag in the belief that they were now on the right side of the universe.

The Polish frontier guards didn't ask him anything. Worse was when he was waiting for clearance on the Ukrainian side and two civilians in tracksuits and puffer jackets tapped on his window. They had the name of the capital scrawled on a piece of cardboard and were carrying leather shoulder bags. He wound down the window and through it one of them immediately thrust his angular face borne on a thick neck. He didn't understand the words much but was in no doubt that they were after a lift. The first one was breathing very fast like a fighting dog while the one on the other side of the car was already reaching for the door handle. He, however, had absolutely no desire to share the inside of his car with them for the next seven hours. He got out of it by saying he was only going as far as the nearest town. As he set off, the Ukrainian gave his roof a couple of farewell thumps.

Once past the frontier, he stopped for a pee by the roadside. So this was Ukraine. What was he doing here? He'd known beforehand that in the morning everything would look different from the evening before. That was why he'd wanted to set off at night. Had he been lured here in pursuit of adventure? More likely to discover what, if any, adventure might follow pursuant to that allure. He had to admit to not having the foggiest idea of how he might shape up. And that was the one thing about it that had drawn him on.

In the opposite direction there was a long queue of cars and alongside them people who'd set off on foot. He was surprised at how little there was that could be said of them. At first sight, they looked no different from people queuing outside a shop that was holding a closing-down sale. Migrants from the Middle East were unlucky in that everything about them con-stituted a distinct category of mankind: refugees. These people only looked like frustrated, perhaps rather tired customers. They were lucky to look like us.

He stopped again. He took a baguette and waited for a car going in the opposite direction to pass, then he tried to offer it to a woman wearing a purple coat. She kept shifting from one foot to the other—most likely the high boots she was wearing had very thin soles—and her cheeks were aflame with frostbite. The lady declined his baguette, but her son reached out a mit-tened hand for it.

So much for that then. On the screen, the cameras hidden in the bodywork showed him frost-coated fields to the right and a line of frozen people to the left. When his satnav came back to life, it assured him that the traffic ahead was unlikely to be heavy.

*

At the Lviv bypass he hesitated—should he head for the city centre or just keep going? He knew that, for now, Lviv was not affected. Some priest had boarded up a church's windows and secreted the icons in the crypt, and the city was overburdened with fugitives, nothing beyond that. It made better sense to carry on, but it was eight in the morning, exactly the time when he would turn on the office coffee machine every day and immediately start cursing his assistant for having started buying some sour-tasting variety.

So he weaved his way through the suburbs and parked outside a long building that sported a blue-and-yellow flag. Three times he checked that it was all right to park there, and twice he checked that he had locked the car. He sensed that leaving an unlocked car to which nothing could possibly happen was the highest drama that could befall a man in his position.

He looked about him. It was a frosty winter morning. In one corner of the square someone had lit a fire in an old barrel and a group of people were warming their hands at it. For a moment he looked at them: there was something primordial about it. Except for that open fire it all seemed so familiar—were it not for all the shop signs in Cyrillic he might have thought it had all been a dream. The start of a new day, with him heading for all those box files, paper files and computer files waiting for him in his office.

He found the nearest coffee bar and sat at a slightly scruffy table. He gave his order in English, and when the waitress came back she asked him if he was a journalist. He nodded so as not to have to think up some alternative. She thought it important that the Western media were keeping a record of what was going on—if only it might reach people in Russia as well. He took a sip of coffee and nodded again. He liked the look of her, but there was nothing to be done about that. Through the window he saw a patrol armed with submachine guns, while outside the hairdresser's across the street there was a woman with a head full of curlers smoking, round her shoulders a white cloth, looking bloodstained with hair dye.

When he returned to the car, he found his front wheel had been clamped. He couldn't believe he'd misreckoned the reserved spots, or that they could be bothered with such things at a time like this. It looked pretty much like a sign that he should abandon his trip, but the world is full of signs that each interprets as he will. He tapped out the number on the ticket, but the operator didn't speak English and sounded a bit ratty that anyone should think he might. He stuffed the ticket in his pocket and went back to the coffee bar.

There was a different girl behind the bar; his was sitting on a high stool on the public side and reading the news. 'Block of flats on a housing estate, the Russian army's prime target,' she said, pointing bitterly at the scenes on her laptop. She didn't look the least bit surprised to see him back, they all come back. 'Are you a photojournalist or a writer?' He just tossed his head vaguely and explained what had happened. She picked up the phone and gave the operator a surprisingly brusque earful. Then she wrote her own number on the ticket, just in case, she said.

Ten minutes later, after they'd removed the clamp, they recommended that next time he put a sign behind the windscreen bearing the legend *PRESS*.

He extricated himself from the city centre and made his way back to the E40. But suddenly it got harder to drive, as if the accelerator were fighting back against his foot. He knew it for what it was—nothing spoils a fellow's good mood so much as a pretty girl with whom he has nothing in common. How stupid of him to pop into Lviv for breakfast. Was he a tourist or something?

After fifty kilometres he was stopped by his first military checkpoint. It crossed his mind that he might stick to his new identity as a Western newsman, but it dawned on him that this time that wouldn't work, because he had none of the equipment or ID that would require. And so he told the truth, that he was going to Kyiv and had no idea what he would be doing there. 'Kyiv?' queried the face-guarded and helmeted soldier, looking dubiously inside the car with its creamy-white leather seats. 'Glory to Ukraine,' he said, as convincingly as he could, in Ukrainian, and hoped that would do. 'Glory to our heroes,' the soldier mumbled.

*

The number of checkpoints rose steadily. At one of them he remembered, quite out of the blue, that that girl in his class had been called Lázničková, Alena Lázničková. They went out together once, were seen, and next day it had all gone embarrassingly pear-shaped. After that he stopped paying her any kind

11

of attention and had eventually even forgotten her surname. He'd recently read somewhere that Russia was like a classroom bad boy who beats those weaker than himself while the rest just look on. His own recollection, however, was that if he was being done over at primary school, the rest didn't just watch—they cheered!

The journey was getting slower and slower and he was starting to feel quite knackered. On the instrument panel a warning light lit up, but he'd no idea what it meant, though fortunately it was only orange. Just to be on the safe side he put his mobile on charge.

He still had about fifty kilometres to go when he heard his first explosions. They were coming from the left. With the control on his steering wheel, he changed the scale of the map—all roads north of his came in from Belarus. Somewhere there was an endless, stationary Russian convoy, the tapeworm that they'd been showing non-stop over recent days from satellite images.

He passed several burnt-out wrecks from an armoured column, hauled aside to the edge of the road. One light armoured transporter had, in all likelihood, been done for by an anti-tank grenade, and one of the shot-up vehicles had its tyres completely frizzled. There were more explosions and a little later the sound of distant gunfire. It all sounded different from what he'd heard in his home cinema.

He braked as he joined another queue of traffic; up at the front it was being combed through by soldiers. He tapped his fingers on the steering wheel and for the first time he felt like turning back. If he'd wanted to lend an ear to some other self, it had had plenty of time to say something. Yet throughout those 1,200 kilometres it had come out with not a dickybird. Maybe it was high time for him to start acting sensibly, head back home and send 30,000 crowns to People in Distress. Even fifty thou would be a good price to pay. He didn't doubt that two or three of his colleagues had already paid as much.

At earlier checkpoints he'd discovered that it was best to say what everybody else was saying: I've got family in Kyiv and I'm going to pick them up. Most of the time no one batted an eyelid that he didn't speak Russian, let alone Ukrainian. Just once he had to explain that his wife worked in Prague, but a month before she'd gone home to Kyiv to look after her sick father. She was there with their daughter and he had to get them all away to safety. Now he imagined it all being true, imagined that, waiting there in a traffic jam outside Kyiv, he did have a wife and daughter. Otherwise he wouldn't be there.

After an hour it was his turn at last. Beside the edge of the road there were piles of sandbags and the crash barriers were lined with Czech hedgehogs. Some volunteers were offloading more of the same. Just in case, he'd got some photos of his brother's family ready, but the check was anything but thorough. The soldiers looked exhausted and he drove through without a hitch.

By now, he knew that the queues at checkpoints were deceptive: beyond each one all cars simply evaporated. The empty three-lane highway, straight as a die, first led between patches of bare woodland, then twenty-storey tower blocks began to leap out of the ground. It was five-thirty and the setting sun bounced off the metal surface of a stripped billboard, dazzling him briefly.

On one he spotted the frequency of Radio Relax and tried in vain to tune in to it. The road had now become four-lane and in addition to the tower blocks was now lined with older tenements as well. He couldn't imagine what the fighting would be like here. The straight, wide arterial road seemed just made for parades of heavy armaments, but every block of flats could become a nest of snipers. There were enough tactical obstacles for tanks to come a cropper before they could break through them.—But what did he know about such things? For now he must resign himself to knowing nothing about anything. Even less about himself. That was the first bit of good news.

Close to the city centre, he found an underground car park that was yet to become an air-raid shelter. It was easier than he'd expected, the admin section being a gaping void. He drove underground and parked in a corner. It still mattered to his old self that his car was safe.

He sat a moment longer with his hands resting on the wheel. He lay his head back and right above him, set there into the car's ceiling, was the red panic button. He'd forgotten it was there, he'd never used it. But he remembered what it said in the handbook: in case of an emergency, just press it and someone will come and resolve all issues. The very idea made him smile.

He locked the car and left the car park. In his pocket he still had the Lviv barmaid's phone number—in case someone needed to be informed he was still alive, in case someone needed to be informed he was no longer alive.

Darkness had already descended over Kyiv. He had to find the right queue to join before he got mistaken for a saboteur. Mistaken? At forty-five you have, if you mean to survive, to sabotage your own self.

An earlier version of this story appeared under the title 'Panic Button' in Sándor Jászberényi (ed.), *Faith*, vol. 1, issue 03 of the *Continental Literary Magazine* (2022), pp. 10–19. The change of title was to bring it into line with the others in the present collection: here each title was to consist of one word only (private communication from the author to the translator).

Glue

'Nika, oh bugger, Nika, wake up,' he shook her violently by the shoulder, 'd'you know where Denis is?'

Course she knew. Denis had been her boyfriend for at least a fortnight or so, meaning ever since Sergej had skedaddled . . . She weren't that far out of it.

'Nika, oh bugger, Nika, I'm not askin' who! Where? So where is 'e?'

Where? She tried to drag up from her memory where she'd seen him last and what came back to her was his warped features after he'd come inside her. Then they'd done it again at some stage . . . no, this was all too hard going, the glue had jumbled her memories messily together, she'd got everything in a warp and deep under water. She herself was all under water.

When she came to a few hours later, everything was a bit more ordered. She rubbed her eyes, sat up and Ivan poured her a cuppa, hot tea, hot black tea. Ever since we'd got hold of that bottle of propane-butane, things had been a bit different, a propane-butane gas bottle was high on anyone's list of luxury gear, just behind a hot-water pipe with a tap cut into it and on a par with tapping the electricity mains. We could even cook stuff, or at least heat something up, just so's you get the picture. Definitely better than under a bridge somewhere.

'Nice, is it?' Ivan asked.

She smiled at him and held the cup to her cheek, to give it a bit of warmth. She needed a pee, but she couldn't abide the stinking rat-hole right at the back, used by absolutely everybody, with not everybody even bothering to use their own corner 'cause the room didn't have that many corners anyway.

She could feel her cheeks firing up from the hot tea. In the living room next door there was even a mirror on the wall, but it was too soon for that, too soon for her to look at herself, let alone put some make-up on, it was quite pointless doing anything of the kind before midday and likely pointless doing anything of the kind at all. She glanced at Irina, just a quick check, she was sitting back to the wall reading a book, arms bent, a comic book she'd found next to a skip, beside her was Lia, puffing away at a ciggy and looking at something on her mobile, probably just photos, 'cause there was no signal down there, or some old text messages from her sister, who'd disappeared from the face of the earth, typical, that sister of hers.

Ivan's a good lad, made her that tea, he had, she ought to say something to him.

"Ave any nice dreams today, Sniffy?'

He nodded eagerly.

'What about?'

'Can't remember,' he said and scratched the inside of his ear. This was a habit of his, forever scratching himself somewhere, then sniffing his fingers and sometimes even licking them. Hence the nickname, Sniffy, aka Ivan the Smellible, everyone took the piss out of him 'cause of it, but you know what? It's not that bad a thing for someone to have a liking for themself.

The curtain in the middle of the wall opposite stirred and in came Nikita. He was the only one with a room to himself, which says something, you guessed right there. Slightly older than the rest of us, he was, going on thirty, and he had a record for criminal misconduct—that's what he called it himself, as if the grander the phrase, the better it made his wheeling an' dealing look. Anyway, he was pretty much in charge here and Nika respected the fact, just like all the rest of us 'cept her ex, Sergej, who'd had an issue with it and scarpered, like I said before. I reckon Nikita weren't bad for being the one in charge, he minded about us and looked after us, like now he was worried about not knowin' Denis's whereabouts, aha, I get it, it dawned on Nika, it'd been him, no less, shaking her by the shoulder first thing.

"E were out all night,' he said, squatting down beside her, 'bit odd that, eh?'

She tried to gather up those bits of yesterday, glue that broken vase back together. But for memory purposes glue's about as much use as acid for a dicky stomach, days get glued together stiff as plywood and there's no way of getting time to flex. She struggled like mad then finally remembered she'd pro-bably last seen Denis after dinner the night before, when they'd been having a smoke behind the boiler house, he'd stubbed his fag out and declared it was time to take off and 'go shoppin''. That could've meant badgering a warehouseman for some things to eat that were past their sell-by, or nipping into a drugstore to nick some more glue for their weekend 'conference', or something completely different.

'Your phone charged?' Nikita asked.

'I'm out o' credit.'

'I'm not askin' about your credit. Just pop outside an' check if 'e's sent you a message. Move it!'

Sniffy gave her a smile of encouragement, the poor guy loved her. She scrambled out of her blankets, tossed her old leather anorak round her shoulders and, after all, did pause to glance at herself in the dingy mirror. Her ginger-tinted hair had grown out by now and was showing brown next to her scalp, as if some different hair had done the dirty on her. The last time she'd done it, Lia had helped with the colour, her new aura, giving her head a coating of gleaming copper wires and a real breath of fresh air.

The only light was at the back; along the passages that led outside you had to light your way with a head torch. The heavy metal door that led into the house, well, we never used that so the flat-dwellers wouldn't find us out. We came and went through a little window. At first sight, it looked barred, but it could be lifted out, bars an' all, and if you had the knack, and, believe me, we all did, it never took you more than thirty seconds. Nika prised herself up onto the sill and slipped through it like a cat. She pulled the collar of her leather anorak up tight round her neck, rummaged in her pocket for her mobile and switched it on without looking.

She made for the boiler house. Nikita was forever going on at us about not hanging around too close to the window. At our previous quarters that was exactly how they'd hit up on us, we hadn't been nearly careful enough and some old geezer, who grew vegetables on his balcony, got wise to us.

She waited for any message that might arrive in her pocket, but when a bleep eventually came she thought she'd rather light up before reading it. And anyway Buggy-Boy was coming.

'You walkin' the dog?' she said with a wink.

'Just a quick stroll round the block, my batteries 'ave nearly 'ad it.'

Buggy-Boy was Sniffy's best mate, like Nikita and Denis, they knew each other from kids' home, only a different one. Buggy-Boy, that's what we'd always called him, and it didn't bother him one bit. He would tell everyone how, as a kid, he'd always been dying to have a dog, their family'd gone completely down the toilet, as only a family can, so he'd ended up in a kids' home, where having a dog is obviously out of the question, except for lunch maybe. But the first and last time his stepfather came to see him, he brought him a remote-controlled toy dune buggy. Said it's pretty much like a dog, you can take it outdoors an' it'll be ever so obedient, the signal works up to almost fifty metres away, longer than a lead, so you 'ave fun with it, lad. At first, Buggy-Boy'd been horribly disappointed, but he'd got used to it so quick that now he'd never even consider swapping his remote-controlled buggy for a drooling dog. Whenever he went outdoors, he always took his buggy with him, driving it along the street ten metres ahead of him, and when it ran out of juice, he'd hug it to him.

'Listen, you seen Denis?' Nika asked him.

Buggy-Boy shook his head and flicked the joystick.

'Ain't seen a living soul, is it Sunday or summat?'

'More likely Thursday or Friday, no? But you know 'ow time passes me by.'

He waved her a See-you-later. Nika lit up and fished her phone from her pocket. Nothing from Denis, only another one from her mum, asking if she was okay. Though why she bothered . . . Nika looked round to see if anyone was coming, but Buggy-Boy'd been right, it probably was Sunday by now, not a soul in sight, so next to the only birch tree around she squatted down unmolested and peed to her heart's content on the frozen ground.

*

The very next night we were woken by a banging noise. Like when you hammer a nail into a hard bit of wood, a knot, say, till it comes out the other side. Sniffy was a poor sleeper, so he had his eyes open first, but he was too diffident to reach across and nudge anyone else. Next to wake up was Irina, she and Lia shared one big mattress taken from a double bed, until, that is, Nitika went and demanded Lia for himself; he liked, in sleeping terms, to alternate the focus of his attentions. So Lia also woke, she placed an ear to the wall and concluded that the banging could only bode ill. She hauled herself out from under her blanket and thought it better to get Nikita up, because it was safer to have woken him unnecessarily than not to have woken him at all. After which, Nikita took charge of the others.

He at once started barking out orders.

The girls began hastily shifting everything into the one room that could be locked, while Buggy-Boy was sent off to investigate. It didn't take a genius to work out that out there at the front someone was hammering at the heavy metal door. The door we never used, the door we'd made extra secure by welding to it an L-shaped section set into the wall to stop any flat-dwellers coming to visit. Buggy-Boy rushed back, panting, someone was using something very heavy to try to bash the door in. And there wasn't just the one of him.

Nikita ordered Lights out! Except in the dark the banging reverberated even worse. 'Right then, looks as if we'll all 'ave to go an' take a look together,' he said somewhat ominously, like he had, somewhere inside him, a taut string that he'd just plucked.

There were about fifteen of us all told. I've already named some of them, I might get round to naming more of them in due course. That meant that there were enough of us not to have to be afraid, though we sort of knew the law wasn't on our side, the law never having been on our side. Half of us had no papers, several were wanted because of running away from kids' homes or reformatories or nicking something somewhere, or both, or something even worse, and only the lucky ones, like Nika, had somewhere to go back to if need be. If we occasionally got into a clash, there was no great danger, it wasn't that we didn't know how to look after ourselves, but because we'd never been able to show our faces much anywhere.

In the darkness, we gripped one another's shoulders and proceeded slowly along the rubbish-filled passages towards the noise. Boom, boom, boom . . . and the rumbling that made your temples vibrate. Nikita led, I was holding on to Nika and Buggy-Boy stumbled along behind me.

If ever we sensed danger, we clumped together like a pack of wolves.

We clustered by the door and for a moment just listened to the voices on the other side. Except the next blow was so powerful that it dislodged the L-section from the wall; lord knows what they were using for a battering ram! Nikita switched on his head torch to see how the door was coping. It was still holding up, but whoever was on the other side had spotted our light through a crack and started bellowing.

'Open up, you shitbags!'

'What the hell are you up to in there?'

'Look smart, you bastards!'

Nikita looked from one of us to another, but with that torch on his forehead all he did was blind us all—which tells you something about the limitations of our bonding. He spent longest gawping at Danilo, who was renowned for talking his way out of anything. Whenever a problem was looming and there was no escape, he became our sort of press officer. But this time he kept stonily silent.

'We know you're in there!'

'And what do you want?' Nikita asked after a brief pause, revealing he really wasn't a great public speaker.

'What do we want?' This time it was a woman's voice.

'Let us in, for God's sake!'

With the best will in the world we could make no sense of this. Why would any flat-dwellers want to enter an unused cellar at five in the morning?

'Let us in, sod you, this is war!'

You'll probably find this a bit bonkers, but we honestly thought the occupants had declared war on us and had come to tell us as much. The buggers had somehow figured out we'd taken over their cellar, waited till we were asleep and set out to attack us.

It wasn't that much of a surprise. We'd been in the wars forever and all we'd ever known was kicks up the arse. Let me give you a brief run-down: Buggy-Boy was bullied at his orphanage, once they'd even ripped the wheels off his buggy and stuffed them inside a compost heap. Sniffy got the livin' daylights beaten out of him at home, and with no daylights left they booted him out into the street. Lia was almost strangled to death by her pimp, or whatever the name is these days for them as run porn chat sites, and her sis vanished from the face of the earth, like I've already told you. Irina fell foul of her half-brother, I'll tell you more of that later. As for what I've been through, the less said here, the better.

'We're not looking for a fight with you lot.' That was Danilo, who'd gathered himself together and who honestly, by our standards, was an exceptionally talented diplomat, 'but the cellars are our territory. Leave us in peace and nothing's gonna happen to anyone.'

None of them on the other side said anything, so Danilo added, a bit solemnly: 'We're your neighbours.'

'Listen to that cretin!'

'Open up, smartish, war's broken out with Russia.'

'Druggies!' Boom, boom, boom.

'That's bombs falling, you morons!'

They were talking over one another, all in quite a flap, and we, briefly caught on the back foot, said nothing. And it was only now, in that silence, that we could hear that the crashes were coming from further off, given that no one was banging on the door any more. The noise in the distance that had woken Sniffy. Explosions.

'War with Russia?' Nika whispered. 'A proper war? Against who?' She was from across the frontier, from Belgorod, and simply couldn't get her head round it, so you can stop laughing at her, you of all people! And I reckon she wasn't the only one.

'This place is already taken,' Nikita declared, having put two and two together. 'And stop tryin' to break this door down, we've got iron bars and knives.'

'This is our territory now,' Danilo added.

Long story short, they banged on the door a couple more times, then they withdrew. For a moment we breathed easier, though it was obvious we didn't have a chance anyway. They'd send for the cops, we had an hour, two at the outside, to get packed up. No way were we going to be able to take the mattresses, the propane-butane tank or anything else heavy. I call that ironic: as you do, we'd fitted the place out for this trash, given them a luxury hide-out and some food supplies, and now what we couldn't take with us, we were leaving behind, for that lot. But Sniffy at least chucked what he could into the stinking burrow at the back, leaving the door open so they could find it easily. Nikita was the last to leave, thoroughly cheesed off, he surveyed yet another den he was having to abandon, then he opened the gas cylinder—maybe it blew up when they went to put the light on, maybe it didn't, who knows ...

*

I bet you're wondering why I'm telling you all this. But what else am I to do when they're all completely spaced out? At least things didn't work out too bad today, wouldn't you say? Afterwards you must tell me more about yourself. You really didn't bump anybody off?

Nikita didn't like us all wandering about outside as a group. If anything happens, he says, it's always better to have someone in reserve. Fat chance of that this morning. We needed to clear out and find ourselves a new pitch as soon as poss. But that was definitely all up in the air, cellars were out of the question, none of us fancied being under some bridge, and none of us had any better ideas either. We drifted along past tower blocks, the buggy ten metres ahead of us like in some parody of a bunch of spies, and a ghastly wind was blowing. Danilo suggested we at least take refuge in the metro till we hit on something better.

I'll tell you this much: if I ever have a house to call my own, I'd want the bathroom tiled like a Kharkiv metro station. But this isn't the time to describe that to you. Thing is, down there we were met by something the likes of which you can't imagine: dozens, no, hundreds of people, sitting on the ground, leaning against the wall, wrapped in blankets, some even with a tent, cooking up something on a camping stove in front of it. Whole families there were, kids wrapped in quilted anoraks and scarves and gloves and woolly hats, girls tap-tap-tapping away on their touchscreens like so many nervous woodpeckers, old men taking turns at a bottle. It was like flat-dwellers had suddenly, quite uninhibited, adopted our way of life that they'd been so snooty about before. I call that ironic as well: all your life you've been lectured on how you've failed to adapt, then one fine day they all adapt to you. We thought it was the joke of the year.

We were almost gleeful as we grabbed ourselves a reasonable spot next to one pillar. Some of us had a nap to catch up on our sleep, Danilo had a chat with some folk nearby and found that the war really had started only the morning before, it was just that we hadn't noticed. 'That's why it seemed like Sunday on the estate,' Buggy-Boy kept blathering to anyone who'd listen.

Nika told herself that if war really had broken out, she ought at least to write to her mum. She scrounged some money and went to buy some credit for her phone. Then just as she reached the top, a message bleeped. It was from an unknown number and said: *pushkin ave, liberty ave crossroads, pls hurry, they've got me, den.* Of course, Denis, he'd completely faded from view. She had a boyfriend, and he might just as well have been dead, she'd forgotten all about him.

'Where the hell's Pushkin Avenue?' Nikita asked when she showed him the message.

'It's where there's that parade of shops at one end,' said Irina. 'Hang on though, does that mean the Russians are already inside the city?'

'Yep, paratroopers and groups of saboteurs,' someone nearby piped up.

'Have you tried calling that number?'

Nika shook her head.

'So whip upstairs an' give it a go, look smart!'

Nikita was in no mind to trail halfway across the city. Except Denis was a mate, Denis was more than just a mate. He couldn't believe he could be so dumb as to get himself taken the very second day of a war.

'No answer,' said Nika as she came back.

'Bugger. Right, you're coming with me. And Vitya. Let's get moving.'

Vitya was something like Nikita's bodyguard, a slightly over-done dumpling. You could tell they'd had a gym at his institution and at any critical moment Vitya would swap one lot of pills for another, then go back to the first ones. He wasn't exactly the sharpest knife in the drawer, but then no one expected that of him.

That day the metro was still running, Nika swept onto a seat and gorged on her reflection in the window. Truth to tell, she was more concerned about her mother than about Denis. On the phone she'd begged Nika to come home, to Belgorod, saying how different things were going to be, a new beginning, just the two of us, I've chucked the moron out, you were right, Nika, he was a total crackpot, but your room is still waiting for you, my little girl, I'll completely remake the bed before you get here, and more gibberish in the same vein. Nika had told her that's all very well, but since it looks as if Russia and Ukraine are at war, it's hardly going to be that simple. 'It'll all be over in no time,' was her mother's response, 'come whenever you want next week, I'll do you some meat dumplings.'

As it turned out, Pushkin Avenue went on for mile upon ghastly mile, as far as the eye could see, and well beyond that, all the way to the edge of the city. They hadn't the foggiest idea where it crossed Liberty Avenue, so on they went, block after block, and at every new junction Nikita swore again. At the sight of armoured vehicles he even tried a feeble joke to the effect that in all likelihood Liberty Avenue had been cancelled.

'Those are ours,' Vitya pointed out.

'Same difference.'

'Look ...,' said Nika, pointing, 'over there.'

29

They looked across the street to where her finger with its chipped nail varnish was pointing. There were a few bare trees, some vehicles parked and a No Entry sign. And to the sign, just imagine, Mishka, there was Denis, tied to it. His trousers were down and he was jerking his head like mad in an effort to get himself noticed. His hands were tied behind his back and his mouth was gagged, so all he could do was squawk.

Can you even imagine it? It was around zero and he was standing there with his shrunken, red, frozen willy and army vehicles driving past as if it was the most natural thing in the world. Nikita had seen plenty in his time, but he couldn't get his head round this lot. What the hell's been going on here? What have the flat-dwelling bastards been up to?

He looked around, but everything appeared pretty normal. They crossed the road and hauled up in front of Denis.

'Haaargh,' he squawked, 'gaarght.'

Nikita took another look round, got his knife from his backpack and sliced through the gag.

'Holy fuck!' Denis unburdened himself. 'Holy bloody fuck!'

Nikita was about to cut through the silver gaffer tape as well, the stuff he was tied up with, but Denis, a worried look on his face, jerked his chin towards the house opposite. A guy in a khaki anorak was cleaning his weapon on the first-floor balcony and watching them with interest.

Nikita at once regretted not having brought Danilo with him: if ever there was a situation that cried out for a negotiator, this was it.

'That's my boyfriend,' Nika took a first step.

'Go ahead and warm him up a bit, I'll watch,' the guy yelled back, clicking the two parts of his gun together.

'I can answer for him.'

'I can't answer for myself, though, pussy-cat,' the guy replied as he checked the alignment of his sights.

'What happened?' Nikita asked Denis under his breath.

'What d'you mean, what happened, you tell me what the hell's goin' on.'

'War's broken out, or so they say.'

'Yeah, I heard. I went out to get some glue for the weekend, right? But all the shops was shut. Three times I checked their opening hours, in case I'd gone nuts. But not a soul anywhere, so I just climbed in through the back, a doddle, at least I could grab more of the stuff, right? An' just as I were climbin' back out, along comes this Bruce Willis wi' another one like 'im, arms shouldered. Sorry mate, I'll put it back, says I, I just needed to glue something together at home. Glue, right? Hm, it was obvious that wouldn't work. Accused me o' lootin', said there were a state of emergency an' either I could go straight to court or pay the price out in the street. Court, d'you realize what that'd mean? So I opted for the street, thinking it meant some kind o' community service, like sweepin' up fag ends somewhere, and by evening I'd be out of it.'

'An' you hadn't done anything worse?' Nikita was just checking. 'All you'd done was nick some glue an' they gaffered you up like this?'

'Me an' my mate tied 'im to the No Entry sign so no queer would have a go at him during the night,' the guy on the balcony explained. 'There's another one-way street over there, so you lot behave! An' don't forget to gag 'im again once you've had your little chat.'

'Hey, that's just not right,' Nika shouted back at him. 'He didn't hurt anyone, right?'

'Who's to say what's right when there's a war on, pussy-cat.'

But then Denis suddenly broke down completely.

'I didn't know there's a war on!' he yelped. 'I didn't know shit about any war! Nobody'd said a thing about a war!'

'We've been over that already, kid. You should keep track of what's going on in the world.'

'Mind you don't come to regret this,' Vitya advised the guy, just for the sake of saying something.

But then suddenly Denis burst into tears. And believe me, you don't ever want to see a lad of twenty-five with his trousers down and tied to a road-sign crying in front of his girlfriend and best mate. I wasn't there, but from what Nika told me, I felt awful sorry for him.

*

You might be thinking that that's where it ended. That I'm telling how the war made us pack up and leave the cellar, and how they caught Denis, who had to stand there, poor bloke, for several days with his balls looking like frozen Brussels sprouts.

Except someone can keep tweaking your ear for so long that you end up sticking a knife in his guts. It's just that with all this going on, something had started moving. I didn't rightly understand it myself at first, but it were like something had shifted beneath our feet, like the bedrock had shifted. It's hard to explain, but I can at least start by telling you that that same day Nikita phoned Boris.

Up to then I'd only known Boris fleetingly and never really figured out what he really was. He'd show up now and again and spend most of the time talking to Nikita. Not that he particularly avoided us, on the contrary the interest he showed was even quite suspicious, but we just couldn't make him out. He clambered into our dens wearing a suit, honest, or at least in a jacket all shiny at the elbows. He certainly didn't look like one of us, but he wasn't a flat-dweller either. He had black, slicked-back hair, a moustache, and it was like half his facial features were missing. Especially because of that problem with his face and the utterly ridiculous togs he kept flicking the dust off, he seemed rather affected. How can I put it? You could tell he was dying to be a good person, and you couldn't help feeling sorry for him. Only recently Lia let on, to me, what Nikita had let on to her during one of her night watches. For a time, Nikita, Denis and Boris had been at the same kids' home, and at eighteen they each went their own way, Nikita and Denis taking to the streets and Boris winding up in an old people's home. A good person indeed, you might say, looking after people on their deathbeds. That's how it works here: just before they release you from your kids' home, they take away your legal capacity and then simply move you straight into an old people's home. That's where they tidy away anyone with nowhere to go, not just those at death's door, but various other poor wretches as well, and they often act as each other's carers to save money. Simply, they needed someone fit and strong and with no legal capacity, someone as wasn't going to be missed, to do all the worst jobs. So Boris had to change the nappies of old biddies who wet themselves, wiped them over so they didn't smell so bad, and even chat to them now and again if they themselves were still up to it. In the end, he would dig their graves, right there in the home's back garden. He had five years of that, when he says he also had to stuff himself with the same pills they gave everyone, to keep them meek as lambs. He got lucky when he was spotted by a lady who used to visit her mother there and who eventually took over from the state as his keeper. After that he lived at her place in some village just outside the city and looked after her house and veggies for her. One time when he'd come into the city to buy seeds, he bumped into Nikita and Denis, after which he'd look in on us now and again.

So, we were living in the metro. Even there, deep underground, we could hear the explosions. Nika opened a new tube of glue, stuck it up her nose and then passed it round. You have to block your other nostril so as to breathe in as much as possible, but what's even better is if you plaster the inside of a polythene bag with the glue.

Except getting high as a kite wasn't really on, the station ceiling being conspicuously low. But even so we nearly missed out when an empty train pulled into the station and just stuck there with all its doors open. Thanks only to Sniffy and his trouble sleeping did we grab a whole carriage to ourselves in the nick of time. It didn't pass without some altercation, but the flat-dwellers soon drew in their horns. We were the ones who knew the law of the street and Nikita knew he was top dog now.

Boris showed up around midday, freshly shaved and wearing a suit, which I reckon he'd inherited from the late husband of the lady who'd taken him in. He greeted everyone in turn, exchanging a few words with each of us like he'd just completed a course in social chitchat. 'How've you been of late, Sniffy?' 'You're looking exceptionally good today, Irina.' 'Your biceps are like my calves, Vitya, that's quite something.' 'I hope I haven't dragged you away from anything important,' Nikita said after they'd sat down opposite each other inside the carriage.

'It's nearly time to start potting up,' Boris replied. 'I've got some jogurt pots ready. Kohlrabi, lettuce, cabbage . . .'

Nikita shook his head. 'It's about Denis.' Then he filled Boris in on the shrivelled-willy situation.

Boris looked troubled and dropped his gaze. 'Like he's standing there practically starkers?'

'Yep, with the pole of the road sign jammed between his bum cheeks.'

This time Boris looked straight at Nikita and for a brief moment something passed between them that they alone understood.

'Hell.'

'Shit.'

'Any ideas what to do about it?'

They were so at a loss that they even considered telling the cops. But Nikita thought that was going a bit too far.

While they were thinking up some plan of action, Irina and Vitya did the rounds of our new neighbours. Irina did the begging, Vitya adding weight to the process. The flat-dwellers, who'd become ex-flat-dwellers, already knew about us and were pretty clear as to what we were, but, with enough problems of their own, they didn't want to make matters worse for themselves. Or maybe they'd just become more accommodating now they were in a like pickle. I'll tell you this: nothing stirs people to compassion like when they're in need themselves. So we took what we were given, and if someone didn't want to part with anything, Vitya gave them a dirty look and they coughed up anyway.

Our six-member squad waited till after dark before heading back to the Pushkin and Liberty Avenues crossroads. The metro had stopped running, and it was a long but instructive trek. Obviously we meant to liberate Denis, but we were also mapping out the terrain because now circumstances had changed. Nikita was most taken by the places where you could join a queue and be given a rifle in next to no time. No one knew what was coming and everyone was taking up arms in readiness.

We headed straight along Pushkin Avenue, Nika commenting on the new road blocks that had appeared since the day before. But as we approached the Liberty Avenue crossroads, we turned left and walked round the block. We hugged the front wall of the buildings and peeked cautiously round the corner.

Denis was still standing there and seemed to be asleep. His head flopped sideways and even from a few metres away it was obvious his limp body wasn't holding up of its own accord. It looked as if the job of his muscles was being done by gaffer tape.

I expect you'll think I'm nuts, but it did cross my mind that by that sign, that No Entry, he looked like some weird kind of Jesus.

Except Jesus had a loincloth and was otherwise naked, while with Denis it was the other way round.

Our plan was no great shakes, all it amounted to was Boris ringing the doorbell and distracting the guy with the gun. If that failed, he'd signal Nika from the phone in his pocket and she'd keep the guy occupied while Nikita and Vitya set Denis free. If anything went wrong, the rest of us were on stand-by.

Boris slicked his already sleek hair, cleared his throat and set off. He had this funny walk, like he was constantly clenching his buttocks, which was easy to see from behind, or it might have been due to his comical, down-at-heel patent-leather shoes. He reached the entrance door, scanned the bells to the various flats, then pressed one of them. He shouldered open the door and disappeared down the corridor.

We were on tenterhooks, Nikita even gave a whistle, but Denis was beyond caring and slept on.

Then Nika's phone rang and Nikita and Vitya struck out.

Mishka, I'm sure you can confirm this: if there's one thing in the world you can rely on, then it's that whatever plan you make, things will always turn out different.

The first problem was that Denis was quite unresponsive, even to being shaken physically. They quickly sliced through the silver-grey tape and he collapsed into their arms like a sack of potatoes. They thought he was just exhausted, but on closer inspection saw that he'd taken one hell of a beating, you might call parts of him actually horribly disfigured. Nikita quickly pulled his pants up to cover them, then Vitya slung Denis across his shoulder and they came rushing back.

The second problem was that just then the guy with the gun came out onto the balcony. At least we thought it might be a problem. If Boris hadn't appeared from behind and hit him over the head with a vase. The guy half-turned to check if it was the big brass one from the corridor, then slithered obediently down against the balcony railing.

*

In my view, it was only then that Nika started to fall for Denis. Prior to that, he'd been just another member of the gang, a guy she was glad to have around for protection if the need arose. While we were still in our den she was lost to the world most of the time anyway, as strung out as washing on a line. But now messing about with glue wasn't that easy, and above all she'd discovered the carer in her. We'd laid Denis down at the far end of the aisle of our carriage, between the seats, covering the windows to ensure his privacy, and now she barely ever left his side.

Fortunately he'd come to on the way, but he was still frozen stiff, shaking all over and his teeth chattering like a little kid's when you haul him out of the water. Boris held him upright from one side, Nikita from the other, regular three musketeers, oh and with Nika as the fourth one. She warmed each of her hands against the other then placed her palms on Denis's frostbitten bottom. She tried to massage him to get the blood moving and was terrified of what she might be going to see when they turned Denis over. He'd got little idea as to who'd made such a mess of him, though the one thing that stuck in his mind was how they shouted non-stop that this prick was definitely not going to have the balls to go looting ever again.

They were sitting in a tight circle at the end of the carriage with Vitya seeing to it that they weren't disturbed. They were discussing something. In the adjacent carriages and on the platform, the flat-dwellers were slowly getting ready for bed. You could see them reading a book, staring into their phones or looking at something on their iPad, some of them with their heads starting to droop. The fluorescent lights were still working steadily, and without a phone you wouldn't know if it were day or night, yet people kept to their familiar routine: 10 p.m. teeth, loo and hit the hay.

It suddenly crossed my mind that they wouldn't have done this to a girl. They'd never have tied a girl to a road sign and pulled her pants down, whatever she might have stolen.

'A girl they'd have hauled off home, tied up and raped,' said Irina with a sneer. 'Why would they offer her to third parties?'

'Humiliating someone depends on who they are,' Lia chipped in. 'No pussy gets offered in the street for free. But a willy's useless, willies have to pay.'

It could have been because we had neither glue, nor a signal, so that evening we started chatting more. But it was most likely what had happened to Denis that set us off. He'd fallen asleep at the end of the carriage, Boris and Nikita rejoined us, but Nika stayed with him, a regular Mary Magdalene.

Lia was just telling us what things had been like at the birdcage she'd been kept in. One warden eyed all the girls up in advance, then when they were to be released, they were passed direct from hand to hand.

'A car drew up outside, them offering to drop me off in the city. They knew what they were about, an ordinary car and, most important, a woman in it. Fat, she was, your real carer type. Said she was from some organization that helped girls like me to get back into normal life, she'd take me back to her office and we'd see what could be done. But the minute the office door closed behind me they started picking me over, I had to strip, they took loads of photos of me and put them on the web. For the first time in my life I were making some money, 'cept it weren't for me. On the other hand, who ever landed a job on their first day out of the birdcage?'

Yelena, I haven't told you about her yet, put her arms round her shoulders. Then she rustled up a candle from somewhere and lit it.

'More another time,' said Lia, wiping away a tear.

'Something similar happened to me, only at home,' Irina picked up the thread. 'My parents got divorced and my mum started changing blokes like socks. Some were okay, but the last one moved in with us along with his bastard of a son, about two years older than me. A stupid sod he was, and he kept coming on to me. But I weren't interested, I were in my final year at vocational school and in love up to my ears. One day when we were at home just the two of us, he burst into the bathroom and started filming me in the shower. Said I could either give him a blow-job or he'd put it on the internet, where it'd stay forever. Except, I didn't have to do it just that once. My big mistake was right at the start, I should have scalded his pig's mug with hot water from the shower. 'Cause once he found he'd got away with it, he made me do it time and time again. Always recording it. So much that the bugger had to buy himself an external hard drive. I knew I was in deep shit. Humiliated and trapped. In the end I just had to run away. Within a week, he'd put it all on the internet, sending out links all over the place just to make sure, and you can bet your life that not one of my so-called mates didn't take a look.'

Sniffy reached inside his tee and scratched his armpit then rubbed the tip of his nose between his fingers. He rocked a bit as he was at it and it looked as if he were about to say something, but he just shook his head, hopeless. Boris cleared his throat and glanced at Nikita. He was staring hard at the carriage floor, his fists clenched.

'It's hard to take what happened to Denis,' he began somewhat pompously. 'The punishment should be made to fit the

41

crime, otherwise justice itself becomes a worse crime. All of us here have had some experience of that.'

Boris stopped speaking, Nitika waited to see what he'd say next, then after a brief pause muttered: 'Is that all? Tell it like Lia and Irina, withing mincing your words. Go on.'

Well, nothing like this had ever happened before. In the den we hadn't been in the habit of asking after each other's past. Now and again, someone might confide in one of the others, but with the expectation that they'd keep it to themselves and not go broadcasting it far and wide. Not everyone could keep control of their trauma with a transmitter like Buggy-Boy.

'Thing is,' Boris began, having taken a deep breath, then he paused again. 'You probably all know that Nikita, Denis and me, we've known one another for quite some time.'

Several of us nodded.

'We met in the Polivino kids' home, me and Boris were fifteen, Denis a year older. At one stage we even shared a room, and that definitely helped us survive the place. The nerve ends still missing from my face, they died there after two older inmates regularly bashed my head against the wall. Don't know why they did it—probably 'cause it made 'em feel good.'

Boris gave a sniff, as if checking his nose wasn't still bleeding, then he went on: 'The Polivino kids' home is on land that includes some woods. And in those woods we could be a bit happier. Denis discovered some magic mushrooms there, and they did wonders for us. And we also used to pee on anthills 'cause we liked watching what happened next. We felt so okay in the woods that we decided to build a house there in secret. We chose one tree at the far edge of the home's land, worked everything out in our minds, but we had a problem, too lazy we were to saw all the timbers we needed using an ordinary saw. The caretaker had a power saw that he kept in the garage. A power saw, just the thing. Problem was, where to get the fuel for it. Any petrol had always been kept under lock and key since some bastards before our time had got hold of it, sloshed it all over the upstairs corridors and set it ablaze. Then Denis had the idea of siphoning some from the tank of the director's car.'

Boris glanced towards Nikita, who nodded for him to go on.

'So we got hold of a rubber tube and a can and waited till the coast was clear. But we were out of luck. At that very moment, the director just happened to pull his blind up ...,' said Boris, running a finger across the candle flame. 'Of course punishment followed: from six in the evening till six in the morning we had to stand in the corridor with our arms stretched out in front. And that was a chance the older inmates couldn't pass up. First, just after lights out, the two who used to bash my face into the wall came along and pulled our trousers down. Then they left, having pointed out that we couldn't pull them back up again, otherwise it would be obvious we'd taken a break from holding our arms out. Even worse, the night warden showed up sometime after midnight, Vasil his name was. He was known for being a deviant, even the director knew but did nothing about it, protected him 'cause he was glad of any staff he could get to work in that hellhole. Vasil plonked a chair down in front of us, opened a bottle of beer, stared at our groins for minutes on end, deep in thought and burping. After about an hour, he told me to come with him and in his room he raped me.'

'Actually, it were me he picked,' said Nikita, finally looking up from staring at the floor.

'No, it were me,' Denis chimed in from where he was being supported by Nika.

'We summoned up the courage to go and complain to the director, but all he said was that we now knew what it were like when someone poked a hose where he shouldn't.'

'What made it worse were that Vasil never stopped.'

'An' to the best of our knowledge they're both still there.'

''Cause we couldn't prove anything.'

'And that swine protected 'im.'

'Who were gonna believe urchins from a kids' home ...'

'When our time were nearly up, they took all Boris's legal rights away and packed him off to an old people's home. There they stuffed him with aminazin and haloperidol, said it were to calm him down. But that muck's worse than glue.'

'For years at a time you're completely out of it.'

'But now we could be in with a great chance,' Nikita concluded. 'So tomorrow, you'll go and report to the home guard militia. That's where we're at now, there's a war on.'

*

We already had one rifle, taken by Boris from the guy he'd hit over the head with that vase, but one wasn't enough. Except not everyone over eighteen and with his papers in order fancied joining the queue the way Nikita had imagined. After all, it meant finding oneself dangerously close to the kind of people we had good reason to avoid. Also it wasn't even all that simple, not just a matter of joining a queue and showing one's citizenship ID, you also had to go through some hasty training and be assigned to a particular patch, where you were meant to keep watch and go out on the beat. Finally Nikita chose Vitya, who was mad about guns, and me and Yelena. They taught us how to shoot standing up, kneeling, lying flat, a woman, they said, had to be prepared to fire from any position. At first, the weapons were made of wood, but late on the third day they handed us real rifles, showed us what to do with them, then we two girls just scarpered. Vitya acted more responsibly, even guarding some building briefly to the point where Nikita was afraid in case he'd really got the bit between his teeth and was ready to become a defender of the fatherland, but he did come to his senses, fortunately, and he too was back that same evening.

In the metro things were going well so far. Now and again a patrol came round and gave us funny looks, but that only happened a couple of times, after which we learned to disperse among the flat-dwellers. Not that we'd have been able to lose ourselves among them completely, street kids are simply all too obvious, though the folk were pretty obliging. Also they didn't have anywhere to wash and they were running out of clean clothes, so they'd started to smell like old mushrooms, they'd got rings under their eyes and some were generally starting to look like old towels. But the main thing was that, after a few pointless skirmishes, they now understood they had to get along with us, share their food when we got hungry, let us use their phones and borrow their charged-up iPads if we wanted to watch a film in the evening.

Our carriage became a kind of control room for the whole station. We'd got our weapons well hidden in the tunnel and we didn't even need to get them out, everything running like clock-work by now. At the cost of some slight exaggeration, I might say that Nikita was like a kind of enlightened ruler bent on thinking up various improvements, while Danilo announced them to the people, Vitya enforced them, Irina and Lia were the bureaucracy and Sniffy contentedly picked his nose. Sometimes, Boris would take a stroll along the platform in his suit, exchanging a few polite words with the flat-dwellers about their latest problems so they felt they mattered to someone at least.

One evening we even organized some races for their kids. Buggy-Boy created a track out of various sleeping bags and other stuff and they had to see who could get to the end fastest—you should have seen the fun they had. Obviously Buggy-Boy would have won every time, but Nikita banned him from taking part, saying that others had to be given a chance, so Buggy-Boy was left checking times and changing batteries. I could tell how happy he was that he mattered for once and that for once he was enjoying some respect, which was much more dangerous for him than if he'd shown them a clean pair of heels and beaten them hands down, as I hope you appreciate.

That week we were in no hurry to go anywhere. The most important things were happening at the carriage's far end, where Denis, in his retreat made up of a pile of camping mattresses, was slowly getting better. Nika spent endless time re-dressing his chilblains, cleaning his wounds and trying to talk sense into his bruises, several times a day she gave him a gentle massage, brought him food, and at bedtime she even read to him.

And along with Nikita and Denis she helped plan this trip to Polovino.

They started calling it their tango, their tango argentino, like they'd be having a ball, if a pretty woeful ball. Arms and ammunition had been supplied by the home guard militia, but they also wanted to take some glue as a favour to the inmates, and they needed a van as a means of getting there at all. So one day, Sniffy, Yelena and Vitya took a trip to a drugstore, but taking a great deal more care than Denis the time before, though there wasn't that much left on the shelves anyway, good thing, really, that people, not knowing a good thing when they saw it, weren't that interested in glue. While they were there, they also collared some razor blades and shaving foam and deodorants and lip-sticks, some of which we flogged right there in the metro and some we kept in reserve. Meanwhile Danilo took care of the van, less of a problem by then with so many vehicles simply left standing in the street, freely available. Danilo helped himself to an Iveco that belonged to some plumbing company and bore the would-be witty inscription *Silikon & Son* across the bonnet.

By then everything was more or less ready and thought through, but Denis still wasn't fully fit. They'd kicked the living daylights out of him. Do you want some details? Nika said he couldn't get an erection, even at night, and when he peed it cut into him as if he were expelling shivers of glass.

One evening we were having another chat. Even Sniffy found his tongue, his mum, he said, claimed nothing smelled sweeter than his little head, but then she probably found something she thought smelled better. Vitya also spoke, and pretty well. Irina added a few nasty details about the guy who'd bribed and screwed her, then put the videos on the internet.

'How about we grill him first?' suggested Nikita when she'd finished. 'Make it kind of a trial run.'

We exchanged looks of surprise.

'What d'you reckon?' The question was addressed directly to Irina. 'A nice little dance for your baby half-brother?' You can tell from that just how self-assured he'd grown those last few days. Suddenly he was cock o' the roost.

They set off that very same evening. Irina and Lia put on the green togs that Yelena and me had been given when we were being put through our militia training, and Vitya also looked raring to go. Only Boris opposed the idea, again making the point that punishment has to fit the crime, otherwise justice itself is made an even worse crime. But Nikita hit back at him, saying how he looked like an undertaker in that suit and that they weren't gonna go that far anyway.

So off they went, just the four of them, a simple evening stroll about Kharkiv, that shitty city of ours, and look, this is where I used to live, what a coincidence. Irina rang the bell, kissed her bewildered mum once and, right there in the hallway, stuck one hand in the back pocket of her half-brother's jeans. Like: I really have tried, but I've never been able to forget your todger, man. He was quite overcome, glad that everything was okay with his kid sister, they're family after all, and he followed her like a little puppy, out of the flat into the corridor, and into the lift, and down into the boiler room, where Irina gave it to him, though with the help of Nikita and Vitya and rougher than he'd ever had it with her alone. Then they dragged him half-dead out into the street, found the nearest No Entry sign, squirted some silicon into his mouth courtesy of *Silikon & Son* and lashed him to the post with gaffer tape in the approved manner of the times.

*

Don't worry, it won't be long now, we're nearly there. It's odd how there can be no movement for years on end, then suddenly things go with a bang. I reckon it's just that you don't see the movement, it's like standing water, but even that rises slowly and puts ever greater pressure on the dam until one night it ruptures and then everything goes flying, the concrete, soil and rocks, and down below creates absolute havoc.

Tango argentino, day of reckoning, D-Day, call it what you like. We woke up quite late, the people in the adjacent carriages were already well on their feet. Only Boris had failed to sleep his fill and now he was traipsing about them, paying them visits like some old gaffer, casting an approving eye on the way the flat-dwellers had fitted out their carriages. Denis was also awake, though he was still lying there and staring up at the ceiling and projecting unimaginable horrors onto it.

We had some breakfast, actually more like lunch by then. Vitya and Nikita then grabbed a blanket and sneaked into the dark tunnel to retrieve the weapons. They wrapped them up tight and added them to the other stuff we meant to take with us, rather a lot of it, as it happened. The van was already waiting in a side street, unlikely to be run up against by either Silikon or his son. There was supposed to be ten of us, the three musketeers and Nika jammed in the front and the rest in the cargo space with the tubes of silicon, rubber tubes and caulk.

'Get moving then,' said Nikita, hounding us into the van after we'd gone over the plan one last time. The van's back doors slammed shut behind us. It was pitch-dark inside and you know what it's like, looking for a torch in the dark. We could hear them still discussing something in the front, boom-boom-boom, we hammered on the dividing wall and Nikita started the engine.

I don't know if you've ever ridden in the back of a van, but the slightest hole in the road really makes itself felt. 'My backside's gonna be beaten tender just right for frying,' Lia declared. Sniffy laughed, but we were all rather jittery really. Only a week back and it wouldn't have crossed our minds to take justice into our own hands, and now we were petting it, tickling it and pinching it and it was writhing at our feet all bathed in sweat. Irina told us all how good it had felt to smash her half-brother's cakehole in and even spit in his face after it was over, and Nikita promised that we were all going to get our turn. Only Boris remained a bit out of sorts as he continued trying to be the right man in the wrong place.

Fortunately, it wasn't far to Polivino. After about thirty minutes, the van turned off down a rough track, along which we trundled jerkily awhile before Nikita stopped and Nika opened the back doors. You had to shade your eyes, so bright it was suddenly, but soon you could see you were surrounded by woods—it hadn't been a track between fields, as I'd thought, but a track through a forest, the last five minutes of which had tossed us violently this way and that.

It seemed the coast was clear. We stretched our stiff legs and Nikita passed the keys to Sniffy, who was to stay put, ready to rush in and pick us up if anything went wrong.

'There,' said Denis, pointing.

We looked where he meant, but there was nothing but trees all around.

'There, on that tree, that's where our house was going to be.'

Nikita glanced at Denis and said it'd been meant to be in a completely different place. It was quite comical, seeing them failing to agree. Denis insisted he was in no doubt, and Nikita said it had been an oak tree and that this 'ere was a beech, while Boris left them to it because he had honestly no idea himself.

'Well, hopefully you'll at least agree on the right warden,' said Nika with a grin. I couldn't have got away with that, but she was now so much one of them that she could take such liberties.

'It's about ten minutes from here,' said Boris, flicking some dust from his sleeves.

'Pick it up and carry it for once,' Nika told Buggy-Boy, seeing what he was about. There was no point trying to persuade him to leave his buggy behind, they were inseparable. And he also claimed it was a reconnaissance vehicle.

We had four rifles between us, Nikita, Denis, Boris and Vitya shouldered one each and off we went through the freezing cold forest. The fallen twigs and leaves beneath our feet made a terrible racket. Nikita said we should spread out a bit, but a magpie started squawking somewhere over our heads and gave notice of our presence anyway. I suddenly felt like we hadn't really got a proper plan, and if it came to it I'd have cheerfully gone back to the metro to choose some tiles for my bathroom. 'Cept by now that was out of the question.

After less than a quarter of an hour, the forest began to thin and through the trees this pale-yellow building with two wings appeared. To me it looked like some old hunting lodge, service buildings to the left and the actual house off to the side, looking like an ordinary multi-occupancy block. On the drive there was a car and a van, but otherwise we detected no signs of life.

Yelena stayed at the forest fringe, to keep watch, the rest of us ran cautiously towards the house and, bent double, scurried along by the wall like rats.

'This is where our room was,' Nikita whispered.

Through the ground-floor windows you could see inside, you just had to lever yourself up a bit on the sill. The rooms were a total mess, here a backpack, there empty vodka bottles, in one bed someone asleep with their feet poking out, from another only a black mop of hair was visible. I'd not seen the inside of a children's home before, but I never expected such anarchy. Nikita sent Danilo and Buggy-Boy inside to wake everybody up and explain that the day of reckoning was nigh. We didn't doubt they'd have their own accounts to settle with Vasil and would be glad to join us.

Nikita remembered that the director's office would be in the lodge proper—first we'd deal with the director, then the warden, nicely according to rank. I don't know if you noticed, but set into the large wooden door made of green planks there's a smaller chipboard one and that's how we got into the driveway and from there into the courtyard.

Still not a soul in sight. Vitya stayed there on guard, Nikita went and stood to one side of the door into the corridor, Boris to the other, then together they burst in. The long shiny corridor ran round the whole courtyard and heaps of doors led off it. Those three might not have remembered the exact tree where they wanted to put their treehouse up in the branches, but they headed straight for the director's door. They exchanged glances, then checked to see if we were all ready, Nikita gave the signal and Boris—Boris politely knocked.

At first nothing happened, then came: 'It's open.' It sounded like we'd just woken somebody up.

They recognized his voice. Nikita nodded, now they were going to dance that tango together.

Boris opened the door and—can you even imagine, Mishka, how confused he was by what met his eyes? The director was sitting bound to a chair, his face covered in weals. It's been a while since I said something was ironic, right? Well, I certainly call this ironic: you've hated someone for fifteen years and when you finally have a chance to get your own back, you find someone's beaten you to it. Some people are just so damned unlucky that they'll even get queue-jumped in the queue to hell.

'Thank God you're here,' the old gaffer said with a sigh of relief. That's how he struck me, an ordinary old gaffer. And that was another surprise, I'm inclined to say disappointment.

But most of all we hadn't a clue what he was jabbering. Like he'd been waiting all these years for us to come and get him? Had he been conscience-stricken and so impatient for justice to be meted out to him that he'd had himself bound in readiness and asked someone to go on and knock him about it while they were at it?

'Thank God,' he repeated. 'Glory to Ukraine!'

'Remember me?' Nikita asked him.

The director looked at him closely.

'D'you remember us?' Nikita asked, pointing at Denis and Boris.

Suddenly, the director's face brightened even more.

'How couldn't I remember you? But it's been many long years, I can't recall your names. You were good lads, though I think you tried to steal my petrol one time. But now you're fighting for your country, we brought you up well!'

'Cut the crap, dammit!' said Nikita, bright red in the face as he crouched down in front of him. He was quite beside himself. 'Does Vasil still work 'ere?'

'The maintenance man?'

'The deviant!'

'Vasil the warden? Yes, he does, but I don't know what's become of him. It's been a nightmare, they came and occupied the place.' Then he lowered his voice: 'Have you done for them?'

By then it must have dawned on Nikita, but he asked anyway: 'What buggers have overrun the place?'

'Who? The Russians of course. They booted everyone out and made this their base.'

I've already told you this once before, right? If there's one thing on earth that holds true, it's that everything will be different from how you planned it. If there's one thing on earth that holds true, it's that on earth nothing holds true. You learn the steps of a tango argentino and you get lumbered with a Czech dupak, you think D-day's arrived, but it's only another Damn Downright Dud of a Day. As we stood there in the director's office like a bunch of cretinous lunkheads, suddenly some voices of people speaking Russian came up from beneath the window. Mates of yours whom Danilo and Buggy-Boy had kindly woken up.

So the training we'd got from the militia is going to come in handy after all, I thought to myself. Except Nikita, Denis and

55

Boris hadn't actually had any such training, and Vitya was outside in the courtyard scraping one sole on the ground as if he was the only one who'd trodden in some shit and not all of us.

For a few seconds we stood there stunned, then Nikita left the room at a run and waved to Vitya from the window to make himself scarce. Most of the pack stayed in the director's office, getting ready for some hand-to-hand fighting, some biting and scratching, but Nikita, Denis and Boris took up positions in the corridor. Nikita hid round a corner and Boris and Denis each occupied a separate recess.

Long story short, it was clear to me that our days were numbered.

I glanced towards Nika, intending to bid her farewell. Perhaps we'd just sniffed too much glue and all this was a bad dream. Everyone has a bad trip sometime or other, or maybe they'd changed the glue's composition. Or we might have tickled justice too far. You know, don't you, what it's like when your older brother lays you out flat and then tickles you and doesn't know when to stop? First you giggle, then you beg, get angry and tears start to flow filled with all of that mixed together. It's a kind of kid's version of rape, your first game of humiliation, your first game of absolute power.

A door in the corridor creaked and some soldiers appeared. They'd got Danilo and Buggy-Boy with them as hostages. They talked briefly among themselves and then suddenly, from his recess, Denis saw the buggy heading straight for him along the shiny floor. He realized it had a hand grenade on board, this lot weren't going to dirty their hands with us Ukrainian trash. No time to wait, so Denis went down on his knees and started shooting like mad, as if an armoured car was coming towards him. And he was successful, shooting the buggy to smithereens halfway down the corridor.

'Don't shoot!' the soldier across the corridor yelped, waving his arms as if his life depended on it.

'You must be a right nutter!' Danilo gave vent to his feelings.

'Could be . . . ,' Buggy-Boy mumbled. And like when some hero decides to save his mate between two hostile trenches, he dashed towards his buggy. But it had copped it. Denis had got it bang in the middle of its front cowling, sending it flying ten metres to be reduced to mincemeat against the wall. We took a peek from the director's office just in time to see Buggy-Boy kneeling on the shiny floor and hugging the remnants of the toy car that had been his lifelong companion. He was squeezing one of the buggy's black tyres like the soft hand of a friend and tears were streaming down his cheeks.

You musn't laugh, Mishka, he really had no one else.

'Sorry, mate,' said Denis, shambling over to him quite unhinged. 'I thought . . .'

Nikita and Boris also lowered their rifles and set off towards Buggy-boy. Suddenly we were all there at his side. Nika put her arms round him from behind and whispered something in his ear. Then from the other direction came your three pals, yep, just three there were. They must have thought us utter loons, some sort of Ukrainian sect that worshipped remote-controlled cars, but soon they, too, were patting Buggy-Boy's shoulder. But he was quite beyond himself, crying uncontrollably there in that long, brightly shining kids' home corridor as if his entire past had come flooding into his head and needed to escape in liquid form. If there's one thing among all the stuff I'm telling you about and that I'll never forget, it's this, Buggy-Boy and the holy relics of his buggy.

*

As it turned out, the Russian soldiers had already spent three days looking for someone to surrender to. They said there were more of them, around twenty in all, most of them still sound asleep after their bender the night before. That's right, eh, Mishka? You used to get up late and you're having trouble keeping your eyes open yet again, you know, that way you're never going to win this war.

We all assembled in the common room to sort things out a bit. We sat scattered about in old armchairs whose upholstery was worn through to the foam rubber beneath, only Nikita remained standing, possibly to make him look more important. Somebody before us had left the television on, and some guy happened to be addressing a load of other people and one of your lot said it was our president speaking to parliament. None of us knew him, except Boris that is, he did know him but hadn't recognized him, so it made little odds.

Denis turned the sound down so the guy wouldn't disturb the business we had in hand.

'It's been three days since we deserted,' said Fyodor, your commander. 'First we just lay low in the forest, then we found this neat little manor house. We discovered it's an orphanage and let all the kids go, though we did have to pacify the director. And one warden who was being difficult.'

'Where is he?' asked Nikita, stiffening.

'The warden? Leave him out of it. Right now we have to settle the conditions of our surrender.'

'Conditions of surrender?' said Nikita with a giggle and he went across to Fyodor. 'There's only one condition and that's that tonight we all get well and truly pissed. Before that, though, there's one thing we have to settle first. So, where is that warden? Come on, out with it!'

Fyodor glanced at the two other soldiers who were with him, and one of them said: 'We parked him in the garage.'

The guy on TV seemed to be explaining something rather urgently. I tried to lip-read him, but before I could make anything out there was a squeal of brakes beneath the window, made by the *Silikon & Son* van. Sniffy must have heard the gunshots and thought, poor soul, that he had to get us out of there, dead or alive. He'd come at just the right time, the supplies on board the van could come in quite handy.

'So: to peace?' said Fyodor, extracting a hip flask of vodka from his pocket.

'Peace,' Nikita said with a shrug and took a swig.

'We didn't even know we were going to war. We only found out when they started shooting at us.'

Nikita replied to the effect that we were in the same boat, that this was a war of them up top and we happened to be as down below as we could be, in a cellar, when it started. But you could tell that in his mind he was already in the garage.

He took another good swig and offered it to Boris. He also dispatched some down the hatch and passed the flask to Denis. Only he didn't take a sip, looking instead through the two layers of glass at the fuzzy image of Nika.

At that instant it dawned on me that the poor guy had fallen in love with her. He was smitten during those first two weeks when they'd shared a bed, and now he was head over heels following her caring for him in the metro. Because of the damage to his nether regions they couldn't make love and that had driven them crazy.

So this is love: when you can't shag someone at the drop of a hat.

I tell you, Mishka, if this was meant to be a trial, then the seating arrangements in the courtroom were rather odd. Nikita had been to check that the warden in the garage really was Vasil, then he ordered Sniffy to back the van in. Vasil was sitting bound to a chair next to the garage's rear wall, Nikita, Boris and Denis sat down opposite him in the van's open back and the rest of us packed in behind them. It was quite intimate and that's exactly what made it so strange. Like at an execution when you've booked front-row tickets so as not to miss a thing.

I think Vasil knew from the outset that his day of reckoning had arrived, but he gave it one last go: 'We have to give the Russians what for.'

'Come now, Vasil . . . ,' said Nikita.

'Hand me some lipstick, Sniffy, be a good lad,' said Boris over his shoulder. Sniffy extricated one from the bag of stuff from the drugstore, Boris undid it and scrawled across Vasil's mug: *I'm a paedo shitbag.*

Denis fished a mobile from a pocket, Vasil's mobile from Vasil's pocket, took a number of photos of him and let him choose which one he liked best. Then he sent them to all the numbers on his list.

'Right, Vasil . . . ,' Nikita began again.

'Sniffy, we brought some shaving foam with us as well, didn't we?' Boris said over his shoulder again.

Sniffy passed him some and Denis said: 'If we squirt the foam up his arse, d'you reckon it'll eventually come out through his mouth, Nikita? I think we've got about twenty packs of the stuff. Though some of it might be gel.'

'We could give it a go,' said Nikita. 'Or couldn't we simply smash his mug in for him?'

'We've also got glue with us,' Boris reminded them.

'We could strip him naked, plaster it all over him and then set fire to it. On the packet it says the glue's a class three flammable liquid.'

'So, Vasil . . . ,' Nikita began yet again.

'Foam, glue or your mug smashed in?'

'More precisely, in what order, Vasil?'

'The glue has to be last, obviously.'

'I'd start with the glue. After it's gone through his guts and belly and up his throat and come out through his gob, we can mark the occasion by smashing his gob for him. And at the end we can warm up a bit round him.'

The worst of it was that you couldn't tell if he really meant it. Only a month before I'd have been certain Nikita was just bluffing, but during that last week something dark had opened up inside him. He had in him a taut string that he kept plucking, but you had this sense he could just as easily strangle someone with it.

'But you used to enjoy it,' Vasil mumbled. 'I can remember how you used to enjoy it.'

That immediately earned him one from right and left. Surprisingly, that shaped his mug into a grin, though a pretty twisted one at that.

'Even now you could be talked into it. First love isn't something that's easily forgotten, eh?'

Denis and Boris had to grab Nikita to stop him lunging at Vasil and making minced shit of his phiz.

'You bastard!' he yelled.

So at that moment it was obvious who of the three Vasil had violated. Suddenly it all made sense to me: down in the metro Nikita had let Boris do the talking because he couldn't have brought himself to do it, and he'd just clenched his fists and looked daggers at the floor. All three had been in it together, even Denis had come hobbling along to support Nikita, all for one, one for all. But at the time Vasil had chosen Nikita.

'No, first love is *not* easily forgotten,' Nikita said. Again he picked up the lipstick, bent down over Vasil and began daubing his mouth. Making the grotesque mouth of a clown, the ugly lips of an evil, obscene clown that took over half his chin with its three-day-old stubble. Then he went back and sat in the van's doorway, picked up a rifle and repeated:

'You're dead right, first love is *never* easily forgotten.'

You could actually hear the barrel hit Vasil's teeth as Nitika rammed it into his gob. 'Go on, get on with it!' he barked.

'Haaargh,' issued from Vasil's throat. 'Gaargh.'

The barrel had gone in nice and deep, my bet is it made contact with the soft palate at the back. At first, it looked as if Vasil was gonna puke, but he had guts and somehow coped.

'Go on, bitch!' Nikita barked. 'Get on and do it exactly like you made me do it to you!'

Vasil wavered only long enough to conclude that the situation wasn't cut out for lengthy deliberation. You could see his cheeks sink as he began to make an effort.

Nikita must have been pleased, because he even withdrew the barrel ever so slightly so that Vasil could get to work on it good an' proper.

'Oh, that's good . . . ,' Nikita sighed. 'Now get your tongue working . . . N-i-i-ice, today I'm gonna come inside your mouth, awwww . . . ,' he whined like crazy. It had taken me a little while to realize he was only repeating things Vasil had always said to him. 'N-i-i-ice, Niki, nearly there, n-i-i-ice, go on, keep going!'

I don't know who it dawned on first that Nikita really was gonna come. Let himself come. Let it come. If it was Vasil, well, he's never gonna tell anyone now. Nikita leapt to his feet, jiggled the gun barrel about between those painted lips like a lever, and when there was finally no holding back, he pressed the trigger.

That's how simple it was.

And at the very moment when Nikita started crumbling at the knees, at that very moment, you showed up, Mishka. Still all puffy, the complete innocent, like you'd been woken up by that single gunshot, which really couldn't miss. You said you were all waiting for us, that everything was ready for a great party.

I was glad you showed up like that and I bet I weren't the only one. All this justice stuff can sometimes be really stomach-churning. We scrambled out of the van, then out of the garage into the fresh air. Good grief, what had all that been about?!

*

Boris and Denis were standing a little way off, staring into the ground. Nikita had stayed where he was, staring straight at Vasil. Was he trying to get a grip on what had just happened? Did he now want to forgive Vasil? Was he regretting what he'd done? Or was he just relishing that bloodied face crowned with the words I'm a paedo shitbag?

Whatever it was, his musings were broken in on by the text messages that kept bleeping on Vasil's phone. Responses to the photo he'd sent round. Mostly thumbs up.

Nikita showed us the messages when he came outside to rejoin us a moment ago. As if to say: See, I did the right thing.

Boris smoothed his lapels and said nothing.

So, Mishka, what do you reckon: Is our Ukrainian glue better than your Russian paint thinner? I'm tired now. I don't know about you, but I've a sense that peace has descended on these woods. Nika's hanging onto Denis and enjoying a slushy smooch. Sniffy keeps running his fingers through his greasy hair and, quite unfazed, licking them with obvious relish. Vitya's hitting on Irina, but Irina wants Lia, but Lia rather likes Vitya's biceps, so it's starting to look like a Swedish threesome. And Boris in his suit is chatting to Fyodor in his uniform about all the things they might yet get planted in time—kohlrabi, lettuce, cabbage, nature definitely needs all the help we can give her so she can give of her best.

Zoë

Berlin, Lodz, Warsaw, Lublin, Zhytomyr, then preferably arcing southward to avoid any major roads, because the E40 from Zhytomyr to Kyiv had become too close to the fighting. Franz would have gone that way, but Juli didn't want to, Juli fearing that Zoë's wait for them might never be brought to an end. Though Zoë wasn't actually waiting for them, or didn't know she was.

They'd set out the previous evening, the previous evening Franz had slammed down the boot lid of the white Audi too violently and Juli, by then ready and waiting in the front passenger seat, had felt the shock wave, and the muscles round the back of her neck had tensed. Why did he always have to slam it like that? It invariably felt as if she'd been attacked by someone from behind. She checked in the vanity mirror that everything about her neat little face was in order, which it seemed to be, the fright having left no mark on it and her features having been restored to their rightful place and adopted the pose that said: I am who I am.

'Sorry,' he mumbled, having taken his seat at the wheel.

'I do wish you'd be more careful,' Juli said with a nod. 'From the outside it might seem like nothing, but inside it's like a cannon shot. Imagine if I were pregnant!'

Juli was slightly built, as people said of her, especially if she happened to be walking next to Franz, who was almost two metres tall and sometimes felt quite awkward about his superior height. She, however, believed she was superior to him intellectually; after all, she'd made it into higher education, and even now she was doing extremely well at the university. She was an exemplar not of emancipation but of the evident self-assurance with which young women were taking over from their older male colleagues at German universities.

Of course, that's not the sort of thing to be spoken aloud within a relationship—who's superior to whom. They had to be equals; that was the first commandment. And the second was: to exploit, as right-thinking people, each other's strong points, not their weaknesses. Franz imparted to Juli the composure that sprang from his simple physical strength, which he never abused, while Juli helped Franz surmount the limitations of his pedigree, as she once put it, not in his hearing, of course, but to a female colleague at the Department of Politics. What she meant was that Franz came from a small provincial town and worked as a civil engineer, for a year now as a manager at a building contractor's. So while he was making good money, some of the latest departures in the matter of Weltanschauung had rather passed him by. He'd eventually grasped the difference between sex and gender, but had so far failed to appreciate that gender could take a dozen different forms; he had mastered the abbreviation LGBT, if only passively, while Q+ remained a total mystery to him. Whenever Juli got a little tipsy at a book launch and he was seeing her home, she felt like a sculptor gradually carving her own rough-hewn David from a block of stone.

Franz manoeuvred his way out of the line of cars parked along the quiet Schlegelstraße. Two years previously they'd bought a flat here with a vague notion of the family that might people it one day. The vague notion of themselves as a family.

Juli knew full well that they wouldn't be saying much during the journey. Unlike her, Franz concentrated totally on his driving, both hands on the wheel, eyes fixed firmly on the road ahead. In the past she'd tried to start a conversation on a motorway, but his responses were abrupt, like those of an intercity coach driver disturbed by a passenger, and this was one feature of his in which she'd failed to effect any change. She blamed it on the long-distance drives he used to do for work, and now in the car he was used to immersing himself in his own thoughts or at best listening to a recording of some thriller or other. He had no problem with someone talking to him, but he himself simply said hardly a word.

Never mind, they'd been over all that a hundred times before.

In the last couple of days they really had been over all the possible variants: They'd wait for the situation to calm down. Franz would make the trip alone. They'd arrange for someone to bring Zoë to the frontier. They'd approach Médecins sans frontières or some organization like it. They'd make their

Ukrainian agency take care of the whole thing—after all it was their country.

In a moment of weakness he'd asked her if they really needed all this. She gave him a close look and decided not to tick him off for it, at least not right then. She did realize, she couldn't have failed to realize, that it must be just as hard for him as well. Two years previously, when they'd started talking about having a baby, his huge frame had simply wanted to enter her and come. She had fully understood how he was looking forward to it after all those years when their lovemaking had ended inside the teat of a condom. 'I'm going to come inside you,' Franz had wheezed after a party one time, poking his powerful, sticky ox tongue in her ear as if he meant to rape her. Juli had yelped and thrown him off her. Or rather, he had lifted himself off her in alarm and she had wriggled off the bed from under him like a startled beetle from under a stone. She had fled the bedroom, locked herself in the bathroom and begun to cry uncontrollably on the floor tiles.

*

Their approach from the south was not remotely like the approach to any European city. No huge depots, no hypermarkets or multilane highways. Just scattered buildings, in places more reminiscent of a rural environment. To the left a belt of weeping willows, beyond them a vast orchard devoid of any foliage.

Juli bent forward under the windscreen and looked round almost impatiently for any signs of war. On the way, they'd been held up at endless checkpoints and once they'd had to make way for a military convoy, luckily Ukrainian, but even Franz had noticed, and remarked as much out loud, that the fighting was nowhere near as visible as in the German media.

For two days now the latter had spoken of nothing else. And Juli herself had added her own grist to the media mill. Conscious of her obligations as an intellectual, conscious of her debt to society, she had written a commentary for *Die Zeit*, in which she had stressed how Germany's decision to support Ukraine militarily was a truly groundbreaking step. 'We have taken time to purchase our responsibility,' she claimed, 'but now Germany has finally emerged out of the shadow of its own history, which has so far served us as a kind of alibi for non-engagement.' She even wrote that 'acting or failing to act for too long on the basis of guilt ultimately amounts to the commission of further, albeit passive, violence', though in the end she'd had to drop that wording because of objections raised by the editor.

The moment the commentary appeared, she posted it on Facebook and a lively debate broke out beneath it, exactly as she had hoped, and it was even shared by people, people who matter, who until then may have barely registered her. Now more and more were seeking to become her friends, but the main thing was: an invitation to join a television debate at which Ivan Krastev would also be present. Quite a hit, objective achieved.

On the way, she'd taught herself the Cyrillic alphabet and now she was spelling out notices that they passed on the road. As soon as she spotted something that intrigued her, she took a photo of it and then tapped it into the dictionary that she'd downloaded before they set off. So she could inform Franz that, at the closed stall a kilometre back, they'd been offering grilled sweet corn. And that next to a crude image of the Russian president under a bar stool it said LILLIPUTIN. He was looking up at a woman's black-stockinged calf and furtively masturbating.

Franz smiled but still said nothing. When he and Juli had met five years previously at his brother's birthday party, he was impressed by the disproportion between her physical makeup and her mental capacity. A victory of mind over matter, he might have said if he'd been given to unbecoming pathos. On that occasion he'd watched as she helped prepare the cocktails in the kitchen, a fragile creature, he thought, a blonde who might even take fright at a blender. The knife with which she was slicing a lime seemed far too big in her hands, and the lime itself suddenly slipped from her fingers and rolled off under a cupboard. Then his brother switched off the music and, over a bowl of nachos and guacamole, a debate unfolded about Syria—at the time Russia happened to be bombing Aleppo, and in that Franz now saw a peculiar symmetry. He recalled how quickly Juli had the circle of discussants subjugated—he could find no better word for it—and suddenly she didn't strike him as remotely fragile. Almost mechanically and as part of the case she was making, she had twisted her hair into a braid, which neatly accentuated her features, and laid out a set of straightforward sentences, one after another, like sections of railway line that she duly traversed as demonstratively as a railway engine.

71

She only stopped when the music went back on. No, she didn't dance. She didn't do dancing, so for the rest of the evening he had her all to himself.

They needed the same U-Bahn to get home, though, if truth be told, it did mean a detour for him. The only reason he saw her home that first evening was to save her travelling alone, because she seemed vulnerable again as he watched the reflection of her face in the windows of the braking metro train, the reflection smudged by the lights on the platform. He was surprised when she invited him in.

Many things had happened since then. He had grasped that the Juli who had subjugated a circle of discussants, the Juli who held forth before packed lecture halls, the Juli who produced commentaries on domestic politics on page three, the Juli who was the youngest member of the Germany 2050 think tank— that all that was her forward picket. In short, Juli kept an ambassador who was her representative and who was usually received with all the honours due. But Franz also lived with her offstage, where he could witness her frustration over a pair of tights, her fury with the operator on a customer-service phone line, or her despair at two o'clock in the morning over a volume of papers that she'd promised to submit, indeed would have submitted because she always met her obligations, if only the contributions weren't being constantly delayed, or if they were worth including anyway once those idiots from second-rate universities did finally turn them in.

His first intuition never actually left him: the knife was too big for her. She handled it bravely, but he was sometimes afraid that it was all too much for her. Only he couldn't reveal his misgivings, lest it be taken for *disempowerment*, one of those words she'd taught him.

Above all else, however, this was the woman with whom, as he gradually came to realize, he wanted to have a child and start a family. 'But isn't it more that I'm the one you've happened to run into at just the age when you want to become a parent?' Juli had asked, swirling her red wine round in its pot-bellied glass. Franz wasn't going to waste time arguing the toss. Instead, he put it about among his professional colleagues that he was looking for a decent flat and within a few months received a tip about the maisonette on Schlegelstraße, just round the corner from the Oslo, their favourite coffee bar, and not far from several parks ideally suited to rocking a baby to sleep in its pram.

At the time, he hadn't known how complicated it was all going to be. 'So what was in your mind? Pregnancy's not a simple matter like replacing the cylinder in a door lock,' his American friend John had remarked—that was the guy with whom he went for the odd drink in a beer garden down by the Spree.

That this baby thing was no simple matter transpired that very evening when they made their first attempt. As we saw, Juli fled into the bathroom and when she let him join her after five minutes' urgent entreaty, he had to face several surprises at once. He wanted to say sorry if he'd been too brutish and hoped she might be consoled; in moments of crisis they usually did negotiate the curve. Except that meanwhile Juli had disappeared down the plughole and he now faced an audience with her ambassador.

No matter that he was sitting on the floor, leaning against the wall tiles. And the ambassador came up with a surprising and surprisingly detailed proposal. Yes, they could have a child, but, for her, pregnancy was too big an issue. In puberty, a gynaecologist had warned her that her pelvis was too narrow. She was sorry, felt guilty about it and took full responsibility. But she'd already had an idea, having done all the research. No, Franz needn't be the least bit concerned, the child would be wholly theirs. It wouldn't be legal in Germany, but in Ukraine it would.

*

At first, Franz didn't take it at all seriously. If Juli had meant to stir within his massive frame a defender of traditional values, then with this idea she'd certainly succeeded. Never mind how many dozens of gender identities there might be across the globe, never mind the next extra letter or sign that gets added to LGBT with every season so that in next to no time it will make an unbreakable password, he would at least like to insist that a baby be born from the body of its mother. He wished for no more, unless that Hertha Berlin might win the Bundesliga, though that was never going to happen in his lifetime.

But Juli was the better-armed in terms of argument. 'Of course it will be born of its mother's body, that's the only way,' she assured him. 'But *mother* is a social construct that can be split up any way you like. I shall be the biological mother and together we'll find a carrier.'

'Carrier? As if pregnancy's like having someone do the shopping for you because you can't?'

'Sort of, but driven by pure altruism, where a woman assents to bearing a child and so assures the continuation of mankind,' Juli acknowledged with an inscrutable smile that could have as equally betokened irony as her having the whip hand. 'Whether the child is her own or someone else's.'

'But I want to have a baby with you, not some Ukrainian woman who'll charge us for it,' Franz wailed. 'You must be having me on, no?'

'Money's not a problem now, is it? We both earn more than we need to live on.'

'True enough! Money isn't the issue! The issue is that we'd be renting a womb like renting a garage or something!'

It was during one of their talks, such as were repeated endlessly over time, that Juli suddenly burst into tears. 'How long have we known each other?' she asked quietly, and Franz saw that once again he had before him that vulnerable girl, like when you've just peeled a prickly lychee. This time she was wearing a shapeless jumper as she sat there in a yellow IKEA armchair, sipping herbal tea, because she'd caught a cold at the weekend during a cycling trip round Wannsee Lake.

She reminded him that he'd never had the guts to ask her properly about her one previous serious relationship. That was true. Franz wasn't proud of the fact, though he wanted to know as little as possible about his predecessor because what little he did know hardly did any favours to his self-esteem, with which he had no problems otherwise. Paul, at forty-two, had been made a professor of sociology at Leipzig and Juli was able to discuss with him the very things that were of no concern what-soever to Franz: performance metrics in an academic environment, positive discrimination in selection procedures, or various strategies leading to the acquisition of academic titles. And he certainly hoped there were no other things they discussed.

'I got pregnant twice with Paul,' Juli whispered, gazing into her glass as if she wanted to steep her eyes in it.

Franz felt he was the greatest idiot in the whole of Berlin. 'I'm so sorry . . . ,' he managed to drag out of himself. But also: why the hell had she never told him before?

'Once in the third month, the second time in the fifth,' she added.

'I . . . Really, Ju, I'm so sorry.'

'Maybe you thought I'm just too idle to be bothered with pregnancy. Or that I don't want to ruin my figure. Not that I've got one to ruin, eh? But I simply can't face it a third time. And I do want to have a baby with you.'

This was all getting too much for him. He hurled himself at the yellow armchair in which she was hunched and aimed his head at her lap. It wasn't entirely clear whether he meant to hug her or just snuggle up to her. The outburst of emotion contained elements of both. For a time he couldn't stop himself, his feelings acting like the cluster bombs he'd just been reading about.

'Motherhood is only a construct,' Juli whispered as she stroked his hair.

That evening changed everything. From then on it was their joint plan, their project shared. First of all Franz taught himself the proper terminology: you didn't refer to 'renting a womb like a garage', but to 'surrogate mother', and a distinction was to be drawn between altruistic, proxy motherhood and the kind you just paid for. The altruistic version was facilitated by several countries, though it often took place outside the law, in a grey area where one friend is moved to offer another to do it for her, to take on the burden of carrying a foetus to term so that she too might have a family, seeing as how they used to copy from each other at junior school. On the other hand, the handful of states that had made the commercial version possible, even tempting foreigners to make use of it, had adopted the relevant legal framework and that in turn had given rise to agencies that knew all the ins and outs.

It hadn't required much effort to discover that Ukraine above all others had hundreds of women going about encumbered with Western foetuses. Ukraine was now not only Europe's breadbasket but also its reservoir of amniotic fluid.

Rates started around twenty thousand Euros. 'That's a good price,' John had remarked after doing the relevant calculations on his mobile. 'On average, a prostitute in eastern Europe costs a hundred Euros an hour. Though all you get is the vagina. Or whatever else you fancy, of course. But here you're blocking the whole insides and for nine months at a time.'

Franz heaved a sigh; of late, John had become quite a pain in the backside.

'And Juli isn't bothered by it? She strikes me as a bit sensitive about such things . . .'

'Twenty thousand Euros is a lot of money in Ukraine,' said Franz, making especially sure he said 'in Ukraine' and not, say, 'to a Ukrainian woman'. And he was not remotely inclined to point out that the greater part of that figure would obviously be kept by the agency. Instead, he repeated the official position of their domestic think tank: 'Every woman has the right to do with her own body as she herself sees fit.'

'As she herself sees fit . . . ,' John repeated. 'And what about social inequality? Or is it just coincidence that Ukrainian women carry German women's children and not vice versa?'

'You might just as well complain that your car gets repaired by Poles and your food is cooked by Pakistanis. Or when did you last cook for a Pakistani family, eh?'

'All right. And have you got her? I mean the Ukrainian woman you're after.'

'Inna?' Franz flicked through his mobile for the message that had arrived a week previously. A woman of around thirty had rolled up her top to reveal her rounded belly. '*It kicks,*' it said beneath the photo, on which the flash was horribly reflected in a mirror, where part of an untidy kitchen was also visible. Franz was afraid John would say something tasteless, like he wouldn't mind screwing her himself, but all he did was give it a careful look before offering Franz his congratulations, if somewhat affectedly.

*

They could hardly have expected their think tank to set those T-72 tanks in motion. In her commentary for *Die Zeit* Juli had thought it impolitic to say that neither she nor her colleagues believed that Putin really would attack Ukraine. Obviously though, when reports began to come in of large-scale military exercises in western Russia, Juli did grow tense. But both the agency and Inna herself assured them that everything was going to be okay. She sent more and more pregnancy photos until Franz began to suspect she'd saved them from some previous round. They also phoned her now and again, despite how her English grated like sand in a poppy-seed grinder and how she always had the radio on too loud. Then one evening, without difficulty, they understood that they were expecting a baby girl, they really were expecting a baby girl.

Franz wanted her to be called Zoë. Like his Jewish grandmother. And also because Zoë meant life. Life!

They followed the pregnancy from a distance of almost twelve hundred kilometres, but simultaneously as if from the next room. Everything was going fine, except that the expectant mother had been given 28 February as her due date. And all they could do was wait because Inna couldn't bring their child into the world anywhere but in Ukraine, or, to be precise, Zoë could be their, and not her bearer's, child legally only in Ukraine.

So that final week they were basically waiting to see what gave first, Inna's waters or Putin's nerves. And then things turned out the way they did: Putin's attack was premature and in such circumstances Inna was declining to collaborate. Zoë came into the world in the cellar of a maternity hospital, one week overdue, and the next day they set out to collect her.

'So in ten minutes Lilliputin garnered two hundred and sixty likes and thirty-one shares,' said Juli. 'And Frieda's written to say we should take good care of ourselves.'

The satnav was showing they were now less than two kilometres from the hospital, when a blackened apartment block appeared on their left. Franz slowed. The house stood a little way back from the road, making it hard to see properly, but the rocket strike must have been quite recent, with smoke still rising from some of the windows. Neighbours stood outside the house, watching as a fire crew in orange tunics tried to bring an injured man down a ladder.

'Are you going to stop?' Juli asked.

Franz didn't even glance at her and drove on.

'I told you to stop.'

'No, you didn't, you asked if I was going to stop. But we're here on a different errand.'

'Yes, but I also need a wee.'

Whenever she started talking like a little kid, he automatically played up to her. 'What, here in the town? Or is what you really want another photo? Playing at being a reporter?'

'Blow you, Franz, I've been into politics my entire life,' Juli replied, turning to face him inside the scented space of their Audi, and it was obvious she'd grown up again. 'And there's a war going on here. I've never been so close before.'

'Just be thankful, there's nothing nice about it.'

'But it's fascinating. Why do you think the entire world's gawping at it? Because they're afraid? Outraged?' Whenever she started asking rhetorical questions he became aware of her superiority. 'Maybe that, too, but the main thing is that we all find it so exciting. Much more compelling than some serial on Netflix. This is for real and nobody knows how it'll end. So just stop for five minutes, damn you. At least we can try calling Inna from outside.'

It was cold and a wind was blowing, Franz did his down jacket up to the neck and somewhat unwillingly checked their surroundings. The house had lost a lateral load-bearing wall and they were approaching from the side that had been laid bare. Juli had a sense of having seen it before somewhere and Franz came to her help, if reluctantly: a year before they'd been to see *One Hundred Years of Solitude* at one of Berlin's theatres. And the director, realizing it would take five hours to capture all the generations of the Buendías, had replaced time with space and constructed Macondo in layers one above the other. The oldest generation lived on the ground floor and the youngest several floors above, and all the action was played out simultaneously. And that was what this exposed apartment block looked like now, like the set for a play that was meant to shock the audience. Juli genuinely found it too theatrical to be really frightening: she could see the back of a bookcase pushed up against a wall that was no longer there, a bureau, a cupboard, a radiator sticking out into nowhere, on one upright wall a pelmet with a curtain blowing out into the open. In one nook someone was moving about: an old man was taking off the wall a clock that had miraculously survived, then he tried to reach a cat bristling on the top of a wardrobe. At that moment a press photographer emerged from the depths of the flat and quickly took a few shots.

'She's still not picking up,' said Franz.

'Fortunately we don't really need her. She promised to have everything signed beforehand. If it comes to it, we can give the food and medicines to someone else.'

'I'd like to thank her at least.'

'Of course that would be better,' Juli agreed absently as she stared at the jet of water streaming from the firefighters' hose, curving in the wind. She now understood that the frightening thing about war was how simple it was. Everything that looked theatrical was really utterly banal.

In the end she couldn't resist and took a number of photos with her iPhone. 'So we can remember the day when we were to see our daughter for the first time,' she said with a shrug, then drew her fair hair back from her forehead. 'So, let's get going, there's nothing more to see here.'

*

It would be unfair to suggest that the agency had left them completely in the lurch. They did reply to the odd email and now and again Juli actually got them on the phone. That was when a woman from the agency happened to have left the shelter down in the metro in order to pick up some food. She dealt with emails from an office set up between a pillar and the wall of the Arsenalna metro station, said to be the deepest underground station in the world, so she felt quite safe there. In some detail, she explained to Juli that she would first write a few dozen emails to clients all over Europe then climb over a hundred metres upwards to get a signal. Their clients were obviously desperate, like one elderly British gay couple who were expecting twins, no less, in Ukraine and were trying to get the surrogate mother in her ninth month at least to the west of the country, but it was all growing so horribly complicated.

Where Zoë was concerned, she was briefer: in a word, they were to come all the way to Kyiv to collect her. She promised that the little one would be all packed and ready for the trip to Berlin.

The drive through the city took an age because of the endless barricades. The closer they got to the hospital, the slower the going became, but finally their satnav brought them to the front of a modern building. The comb pattern of empty parking places told them that the maternity hospital wasn't functioning normally, but they were set at ease by the fact that it looked untouched. From their angle the windows even glinted with the blue, now fading sky, which Juli took to be a good omen.

'One day we'll tell her how we risked our lives for her,' she said.

Franz switched off the ignition and looked about him. So far they hadn't got into any unequivocally unpleasant situation, so her remark sounded more like a threat and he found it rather disagreeable. They undid their seatbelts, glanced at each other and nodded.

Once more they were seized by that ice-cold wind. It must have been minus five, minus ten with the wind-chill factor, that is if anything so namby-pamby as wind chill exists hereabouts, Franz mused. They quickly covered the short distance to the main entrance, but when Franz took hold of the pull handle of the glass door, it proved to be locked. Juli cupped her hands against the glass and tried to peer through into the dark corridors with coloured lines along the walls. Franz rapped on the door with his knuckles.

At that moment an army jeep braked sharply on the street behind them and a man in camo jumped out. Juli was petrified, while Franz felt an acute rush of adrenaline. The man took the steps two at a time and charged straight towards them, shouting something they couldn't understand and gesticulating frantically.

Franz had already gone on the offensive when a pregnant woman started hauling herself awkwardly out of the jeep. Now the soldier was joggling the door and when that didn't help he waved into the camera mounted over the entrance.

Franz let out a deep breath, but mostly to restore his own calm, then patted the Ukrainian on the shoulder. Meanwhile the porter had appeared on the other side of the door, which he unlocked, then exchanged a few quick words of explanation with the soldier. With Juli's help, the pregnant woman went inside, where two nurses took charge of her, the soldier jumped back in his vehicle and disappeared.

So, they'd got in, but the porter refused to let them go any further than the reception area. Plainly, all he had gathered was that they spoke neither Ukrainian, nor Russian, which he probably found a bit suspicious. Or he might have been expecting some financial incentive; Juli knew that Ukraine was notorious for corruption. She fished the file of papers from her handbag and spread them out on the counter. The porter pointed meaningfully at the telephone, which he then put to use, but without getting through to anyone. After five minutes he tried again, as if having had to let the phone cool down or leaving a gap in which they might make him some offer. This time he was more successful, but the only immediate result was that he pointed to some chairs along the wall before returning to his screens: one carried the signal from the security cameras, the other was showing the news.

'I was afraid he was going to pile us into his car,' said Franz.

'My first thought was that it was his wife.'

By now it was almost dark outside, while in the corridor only faint emergency lighting came on. After a wait of half an hour, Franz's mobile started vibrating in his pocket. Before answering, he showed Juli the display, then pressed the speakerphone icon so that they could both hear Inna.

It was the first spoken contact they'd had with her since the birth. Two days previously she'd sent a terse message: 'Baby OK.' Franz had shown Juli the message in the bathroom of the

Schlegelstraße apartment, and they'd silently hugged. Then Franz opened a bottle of champagne and joked that this method of assisted reproduction at least had the advantage that the mother could toast her newborn on the spot. 'And she can also make love right away, being neither sliced open nor half-dead,' Juli added an hour later as she nuzzled up to him.

Now Inna was apologizing in her broken English for not picking up the phone and not replying to messages. Straight after the birth, she'd had to look after her grandmother, get her out of occupied Irpin. Everything had gone well, both the birth and that other matter, though an air-raid alarm going off meant that she'd had to give birth in the hospital cellar, and her grand-mother had had to travel part of the way in a ramshackle shop-ping trolley, which finally lost a wheel, finally, like really at the end, fortunately.

'We're at the maternity hospital now, we've come to collect Zoë,' Juli cut in on her.

There was a brief silence, then Inna said: 'It's good that you've come. I'm also calling now because of that.'

'Because of what?' asked Franz, Inna having lapsed into silence.

'I wanted to ask if you could take me and my grandmother away from here. To Germany.'

Juli looked at Franz. Her rough-hewn David had striven all his life to do the right thing, and in consequence was also naive: if anyone was capable of thinking strategically, it was she and she alone. Of course they could take them, indeed it was now their moral obligation to do so. Though this might also mean that Inna didn't want to give the baby up. And that would be the worst nightmare of all. They had formed an image of a mercenary woman who traded her body, which she was obviously entitled to do, but did they know anything more about her? Maybe this had been her first time and it had left her utterly confused. Most likely she was just a frightened woman who simply needed to be taken to safety. At such a time, that made perfect sense. Except that a frightened woman can easily give in to her hormones, the most certain thing that she has inside her at the time.

'We'd love to help,' said Juli, her eyes fixed firmly on Franz, 'but we need to think about how best to go about it. Apart from that, we still haven't even got to see Zoë. We've been here in the corridor for about an hour, waiting for someone to come and fetch us at last.'

The phone went silent again. Then Inna said: 'She's with me. You have to come to my place and take all of us, otherwise you won't get to see her.'

'Wait . . . ,' said Franz, drawing a deep breath, 'how come Zoë's with you? That can't be, surely, it's against . . .'

'You simply have to come, we're almost family now.'

*

The nurse led them down a long corridor, which kept taking abrupt turns. The hot-water conduit, swathed in aluminium foil, ran along just below ceiling level, while here and there other

pipes dripped away into rusty puddles. Franz could hear a hum-
ming noise from inside the pipe—or could it be that everything
had set his head buzzing? He hadn't slept in over twenty-four
hours, most of which he'd spent behind the steering wheel, Juli
having taken over from him only twice for about two hours at a
time. She did have her own set of car keys, but she didn't like
driving, let alone in places that were unfamiliar. On the other
hand, it had been only twenty-four hours, and he found it odd,
positively disturbing, that you could pass from one universe to
another in a single day.

The nurse strode along ahead of them so fast that they could
barely keep up. She explained she was alone on night shift that
day. Finally, they had to cross to another building where the
babies of surrogate mothers from all the maternity hospitals in
Kyiv had been assembled, because, it was explained, nobody had
the remotest idea what was to become of them. That much was
obvious to Franz: they needed to be held in store somewhere
like unclaimed goods.

'Still nothing?' asked Juli as she trotted along.

Franz checked his phone and shook his head.

'She must have been bluffing, otherwise she'd have sent the
photo, wouldn't she? All she wants is to get us to go and pick
them up, that's why she sent the address, but no photo of Zoë.'

'It's quite understandable that she wants to get away.'

'Of course it's understandable!' Juli raised her voice. And
despite the premises that had underpinned that piece she did
for *Die Zeit*, now, in this basement in Kyiv, she felt embarrassed

as her German reverberated metallically and the nurse looked back in reproof. 'Of course it's understandable,' she said, lowering her tone, 'but we don't have to give in to bribery. And *you*, dammit, don't have to keep telling *me* what's understandable.'

Finally, they reached the end of the corridor. The nurse unlocked the heavy iron door, evidently made to resist explosions, but also, as it transpired, excellent at blocking all noise as well. Through the gap they were now inundated by the sound of babies crying, and as soon as the nurse opened the door wide, they saw a room with around thirty cots packed tightly together along three walls, each one occupied, colonized by a newborn.

Juli gasped. Most of the infants were asleep, but several were crying very loud, demanding to be fed or loved or perhaps returned to the womb, and these hungry and insatiable malcontents woke some of the others before drifting back to sleep from exhaustion. The nurse picked up a bottle of baby milk and started passing from one to the next.

On the table there was another full bottle of the off-white liquid, but neither Juli nor Franz dared offer any assistance. It was all so eerie. Juli remarked that one day they would tell their child how they'd risked their lives for her. It was in that spirit that she'd set out to Kyiv, on a rescue mission that would make at least partial heroes of them, she herself having proved incapable of carrying a foetus to term. It hurt when her friends talked about their problems during pregnancy, by which they meant feeling sick or having a hint of a moustache pop up under their nose. 'I've had two miscarriages!' she felt like screaming at them. 'And the second time it was almost a person!' Except that was the very thing she'd kept to herself, no enlarging on any *almost-person*, and for now she'd also kept the entire special non-military operation in Ukraine to herself as well. There would be ample time for story-telling when they met her pushing a pram in the park. Over the last few days she'd begun to believe it wouldn't have to be yet another trying tale about assisted reproduction that at least evoked expressions of understanding, but a story about responsibility and courage, the drama of a rescue mission halfway across Europe. Maybe they'd seen on Facebook her photos from Kyiv, she would hint, and as she told them, from first-hand knowledge of the facts, about the situation in a country destroyed by Russian aggression, Zoë would be breathing contentedly in the pram and creating her own synapses between her brain cells so as to become, one day, as smart and successful as Juli herself.

Except Juli didn't want to take any photos right then. The twenty or so almost identical babies inside a cellar vaguely reminded her of some sci-fi film. She quite lacked the courage to scrutinize those tiny creatures in cots, marked only by numbers, and try to work out which one might be Zoë.

'Since the war began, you're only the third couple to have come to pick up,' said the nurse, who spoke remarkably good English. 'We honestly don't know what's to become of them. Did you know that until someone comes to collect them they're actually stateless? In legal terms, they simply aren't Ukrainian.'

Franz and Juli did know that, and in all honesty that suited them down to the ground. They wanted a German, just as others wanted a French, British or Belgian child.

'The way it works is that while the birthmother has to surrender the baby, the clients needn't turn up to collect it. We rely on the assumption that having spent so much money, they do care about the baby. But now with the war . . . ,' the nurse continued her lament.

Juli took the file of documents from her handbag and the nurse vanished with them into a room at the back that presumably served as office and storeroom in one. She had left the door ajar, and through it they watched as she opened a fat ring binder.

Juli and Franz exchanged glances that communicated nothing beyond the fact of their presence there. There was nothing about them even to say if they were there together.

'Number five,' the nurse called back to them.

They exchanged glances again, but this time something new had crept in that collided in the middle ground between them and landed with a clink on the concrete floor. Franz took Juli's hand in his and they walked the few paces across to a cot with a purple blanket.

The little girl was asleep, with a white spot of dried saliva in one corner of her mouth. The nurse took a dampened paper towel and quickly cleaned it off as if giving some item a last-minute wipe for the benefit of any would-be purchasers.

'Can you show us the paperwork, please?' Juli asked.

The nurse went back into the office and brought the file she'd extracted from the ring binder. 'She looks like you,' she said, smiling at Juli as she handed her the provisional birth certificate.

Looks like? Franz thought that the baby in front of him looked far more like all the other babies in the room than either of them. Not that that meant anything; all the babies in the room looked most of all like one another as if their features had been inscribed on them by their shared experience. He was briefly assailed by a sense that it didn't actually matter which one they chose. Hadn't Juli talked about how it was only society that moulded most things about a person anyway? Had she not tried to explain to him time and again that we are all but social constructions in cheap clobber from sweatshops?

Juli spent a moment trying to make head or tail of the birth certificate, then half in frustration, half in anger, she turned to the nurse: 'How can I tell from this that this is our baby?'

'I can translate it for you if you like,' the nurse offered. 'But here's the surrogate mother's signature and the agency's rubber stamp. It all tallies.'

'The thing is, we're not sure if our surrogate mother hasn't kept the baby,' Franz joined in to head off any conflict. 'She claimed on the phone to have the baby with her. That makes things slightly awkward, though we don't really believe her.'

'Anything of the kind is quite out of the question,' the nurse assured him. 'As I said, the birth mother has to surrender the child right after birth; she never even gets to see it. That's the basis of the whole thing, as I'm sure you know.'

'Under normal circumstances of course,' said Franz. 'We don't want to suspect anyone, but as I'm sure you also understand, we need to be certain. It might be possible that . . .'

'We have to do a DNA test,' said Juli.

Franz looked at her in surprise and the nurse just sighed. 'I'd advise you to get your daughter away quickly before the city's surrounded, then pay for a test in Germany. Nobody's going to perform one for you here and now, that's for sure.'

'It's our right!' Juli yelped.

'But we just don't have the means. Can't you see we're in a cellar?' the nurse gestured with her hands.

'It's our right!' Juli repeated.

'I might think it's our right not to have our hospitals bombed. And you even have the means to help prevent it. Not that you use them as you might. So much then for your right!'

'And if it proves not to be Zoë?' Juli had adopted a quieter tone, aware, like all Europeans to the west of Ukraine, of her own sense of guilt. 'We'll have the test done in Germany, but what then?'

'It *is* her. She's one of the few lucky ones someone has come to collect. And I thank you for that,' said the nurse in a conciliatory tone. 'You know, things can go wrong even under normal circumstances. What do you suppose happens if the child is born with a cleft palate? Or with a finger missing? Or if the couple split up during the course of the pregnancy? Here in Ukraine we have a special facility where these unclaimed babies end up. You wouldn't want your daughter to grow up there. Take it from me, it's not a nice place even when there isn't a war on.'

Juli leaned back against the wall, then, hands on knees, she slid down the wall and, in a kind of half-squatting position, began to cry. Not with motherly emotion, but because of having finally become overwhelmed by feelings of guilt. How was it possible for something like this to be happening in Europe? Abandoned newborns stored in a cellar somewhere, in a city with missiles landing all over it for no good reason. Children of people who'd always wanted the very thing they couldn't have. And just as she was about to acknowledge herself as one such, Zoë began crying as well.

Franz had been about to bend down to console her, but now he froze.

'There, take that as a sign from Heaven,' said the nurse. 'You're bonded like a mother and a daughter. Sorry, what I should have said was: As mother and daughter, you are bonded together.'

*

In the subdued light of the desk lamp that had been turned to face the wall, Franz looked on as Juli slept. Most likely she just had her eyes closed, most likely she couldn't sleep either but had no desire to probe into anything else or even look at the world. Zoë lay on her chest and of the three of them was the only one apparently sleeping for real. She was ensconced there between Juli's breasts, her head turned slightly towards Franz. Now that he could survey the pair of them at leisure, side by side, he could see that Zoë's lips were the same shape as Juli's, straight, horizontal lips, especially the upper one. In the early days of their relationship, when they were still into kissing, he would annoy Juli by saying her upper lip was like a hyphen between her cheeks.

It had finally sunk in that they really did have a baby. It mattered not how they had come by it. His own huge body had become the body of a father, and from now on it would be shepherding something fragile that was going gradually to grow. He would shepherd it and protect it so that it could grow into its own life, of which, as of now, no one knew anything.

The nurse sat at the desk, alternately making notes on medical record cards or replying to messages on her mobile. Kyiv had long been sunk in darkness, there was a curfew in force and she'd allowed them to spend the night there. Before they bedded down in her office, they'd been back to the car and handed over the food and medicines that they'd brought from Berlin. They'd be leaving first thing, there'd be no chance of giving them to anyone else, and they were sure that any extra supplies wouldn't come amiss right here.

Franz would never forget what happened next. Did a bomb explode? No. From beneath Juli's closed eyelid one lonely tear slipped out, and at that very instant sirens began to wail outside. Nothing else happened, but Juli's tears and sirens were to remain inseparable for all time in Franz's mind, as if the high-pitched whine issued from that very tear as it slid down the cheek of the woman he loved. A tear of Juli's is cause for alarm, he thought, deeply touched. This time the pathos of it served him well.

For the first time in ages he felt truly alive. He gently touched the baby's head, just for the sake of feeling its warmth. Then he fell into a fitful sleep for several hours.

And as he slept, Kyiv was covered in snow.

They discovered the snow next morning, having negotiated the labyrinthine corridors back to the entrance. Franz had Zoë in an infant car seat as Juli said goodbye to the nurse, whose colleague had arrived to take over. There were only a few centimetres of snow, which he easily brushed off the windows, then he switched on the heated rear window to get rid of the coating of ice.

They'd gone barely half a kilometre when the outdoor loudspeakers in the city centre began playing the Ukrainian national anthem. Since the beginning of the war, they'd been doing this at seven in the morning and at midday. In-between, at nine o'clock, a minute's silence was observed for the fallen soldiers and killed civilians. To them, though, it was more like the anthem was being played for Zoë, seeing her on her way from her native city. Who knows when she'd see it again.

'It's horrible not being able to breastfeed her,' said Juli, who was sitting in the back and trying to keep the baby bottle in Zoë's mouth.

Franz seemed to be back in driving mode because he cast just a quick glance at the inside rear-view mirror and said nothing. Juli forgave him, knowing that his sole task now was to get them home in one piece, home and safe. Except the real reason Franz hadn't replied was because he was looking for somewhere to park. The little flag on his satnav showed that they'd arrived, and the Ukrainian national anthem was still playing.

'We can't leave them here,' he said by way of explanation, unfastened his seatbelt and half-opened his door.

Only then did Juli, immersed in feeding Zoë, notice that they'd stopped. 'Where are you going?' she asked, grabbing him by the shoulder.

He turned to face her. 'Look, we've two free seats in the car, we can't just leave Inna and her grandmother here. In a few weeks, this city could end up like Dresden.'

Juli glared at him in a way he'd never seen before, blood flooding her cheeks as if they were about to burst. 'So we can take someone else,' she snapped. 'Take whoever you want, but be quick about it.'

'We owe it to Inna.'

'We owe her nothing. We've paid her thirty thousand Euros. For that she can travel first class to the Bahamas.'

Franz tried to take her hand. 'You know there's no such thing as first class any more. I don't think we need worry. Our papers are in order and we can keep an eye on the rest. We'll just get them over the border. Honestly, it's our moral obligation.'

'Sod that, I know it's our moral obligation!' she screamed through her tears, tears quite different from the night-time ones. 'I know it's our duty,' she repeated. 'I'm German, I've spent a lifetime doing my duty. But now for once I want to put myself first, understand?'

'Of course I do, but right at this minute ...'

'No, you don't understand. You don't understand a thing! Not a minute ago I was saying how upset I was at not being able to breastfeed. And now you want to bring on board a woman whose breasts are full of mother's milk. Great big Ukrainian tits full to bursting!'

'Juli, for God's sake ...'

'It's cold here. Go on, drive!'

Meanwhile the national anthem had ended, Franz sat a moment, helpless, with his hands on the wheel, then he closed the door and belted up. But he couldn't bring himself to press start.

'We're going home. Drive!' Juli commanded. 'We can arrange for them to get away from here somehow once we're back in Germany.'

'Are you coming with me, or would you rather wait here?'

Juli was quite unable to grasp that he was refusing to do her bidding at a time like this. 'Are you going to leave me alone here with the baby? Are you abandoning us this soon?'

'So come with me. We can go together, it's simply the right thing for us to do.'

Juli didn't budge. 'Fuck you! This is your last chance to step on that gas.'

Franz opened the door and looked up and down the street. A cyclist rode by and a handful of pedestrians were scurrying somewhere or other; it all looked safe. He looked up at the building where Inna was supposed to live; at one window someone was smoking, another was plastered over with a Ukrainian flag. He hated it whenever he and Juli were at loggerheads, but this time he knew that right was on his side. They simply could not leave them here.

The main entrance was open, but just inside he was stopped by a bearded man wearing a winter coat over his pyjama bottoms. At first he wanted to throw Franz out, but once he'd calmed down, he obliged by showing which floor Inna Glinska lived on. He saw him all the way to her door and, just to make sure, waited to see what would happen. He left when Inna opened the door and flung her arms around his neck as if they'd been friends since childhood.

'You came, you came!' she said. 'I knew you would. But where's Juli?'

'Down in the car. Are you both packed? I don't want to leave her alone too long.'

'Yes, basically we are,' said Inna. She looked older than in her photos, her ash-blonde hair was tied into a braid and she looked as if she hadn't slept. She stood in the doorway, not knowing at once what to do first.

She was nudged by a baby's crying inside. 'I'm sorry I didn't send that photo, in fact my camera broke some time back,' she said, while Franz groped at the doorframe. 'I know what you must be thinking, but I was so certain that she'd be better off here . . . They told me all the children wind up somewhere . . . ,' she looked for the right word in English, ' . . . in a cellar some-where. I made it my job to look after her the best I could until you got here . . . since you'd been so trusting. Come on in, I was just feeding her,' she indicated.

Franz nodded expressionlessly.

'Let me show her to you right away, she's absolutely fine, a beautiful baby girl.'

Franz crossed the threshold into the flat with a sense that it didn't matter in the slightest whatever he did. One thing was as bad as the next, one thing as good as the next, nothing meant anything anymore. Inna led him into a room where an old lady was sitting in a wheelchair, reaching out a wrinkled hand to touch the baby in the cradle beside her. Her toothless mouth said something to Franz that he didn't understand, and Inna said something in reply that he didn't understand either. All he saw was that emaciated, venous hand on the pink cheek of his daughter, as if death had already stepped up to her cradle.

'Where's your toilet?'

'That door there,' Inna said, caught slightly off guard.

It wasn't that he wanted to throw up. He needed a moment to himself, to pause for thought. He sat down on the toilet lid, stared at the calendar with its picture of endless cornfields hanging on the inside of the door and hid his head in his hands. The best thing would be to take one bag downstairs, leave it on the ground floor, go back to the car and tell Juli that they weren't in. Yes, that's what he'd like to do. Leave as if he'd never been. Except sooner or later Juli would order a DNA test and discover that their Zoë wasn't theirs. If she got it done quickly, she might want to send her back. If she did it later, she'd have no option but to become reconciled because Zoë would have become part of their life. Though Zoë might herself not come to terms with the fact that her parents are not her parents. It might even be she who ordered the test once she found it odd, as a teenager, that she bore no resemblance to her parents. Until she arrived at the warranted impression that she had nothing in common with them.

So he couldn't do it, even if he wanted to.

Would he? He'd be leaving his real baby here, and these two women! Would he be able to sleep easy in his Berlin maisonette on Schlegelstraße? He'd get no sleep at all. Oh, hell! Except if he went down now and told Juli everything, she'd probably want to return the baby that was there with her. But when they got to Berlin, she'd think of her, that baby would be like Zoë's dead sister who'd spent only one night with them, the night of the teardrop highlighted by the siren. And in that case, he'd get no sleep either. Because he would imagine Zoë number one living in some children's home for unclaimed children in a war-torn country and asking herself in the night what piece of brainless Western shit had brought her into the world and why.

So what now? He sank his fingers in his hair. So, he simply had to take them all. Nothing else made any kind of sense. The car only had room for five, but one baby could be on someone's lap, that would work. All he needed to work out was which baby on whose lap. And how about the breastfeeding? For Juli's sake, that might have to be banned completely, otherwise she'd go mad. The babies would cope, babies are tough. Oh, God, oh, my God, he thought and flushed the toilet.

*

They agreed that first they needed to carry the old lady downstairs. Once again Franz's size and strength came in handy, though, just to make sure, Inna also asked for help from the neighbour who had brought Franz to her door. Together they carried the old lady in her wheelchair down to the ground floor and left her there so she wouldn't freeze outside. They carried all the other things down piecemeal, though there wasn't that much. Finally, Inna picked Zoë up and locked the door of the flat, putting one set of keys in her pocket and passing the other set to her neighbour for safekeeping.

And so they came out into the street: Inna with Zoë in her arms, Franz pushing the old lady in the wheelchair, who kept wittering non-stop. Except that his white Audi, into which he meant to load everything because there was no alternative, his white Audi to which he'd treated himself for his thirty-fifth birthday after they promoted him to a management post, his white Audi that radiated the power of honest-to-goodness technology, the cool power that he had been determined to epitomize himself, well, that selfsame white Audi had gone.

And he was so stupid that his immediate dread was that someone had stolen it.

He stood there like a stuffed dummy while Inna dandled Zoë in her arms, having no clue as to what they were waiting for. Zoë was the third baby she'd carried to term as surrogate and now she wanted to follow them to the West.

*

At that moment Juli, with her own Zoë tucked away in her carrier, was passing that vast leafless orchard on the outer edge of Kyiv.

A moment before she'd again seen the masturbating Lilliputin—he'd earned her several thousand likes.

I am who I am, she assured herself in the rear-view mirror. I am a mother.

Aquarium

He wasn't yet quite eighteen, but he got extra years added on by being the son of a hero. One can become a hero in one's lifetime, or posthumously; in Igor's father's case it had been the latter, eight years previously. Hero-father, hero-city, it was obvious to Igor that he was in a right fix. He told himself he was also going to be something of a hero, though he definitely wasn't going to snuff it in the process. He'd be a hero of his own making, not after the manner of his old man.

Because there were still two months to go to his eighteenth, they'd not let him lay his hands on a rifle, only on a steering wheel. And to back him up they'd given him a Valkyrie, a Valkyrie as driver's mate. For several days now they'd been driving round in a battered white pick-up delivering lavash, the unleavened flatbread baked by the local Turks from leftover flour to make a simple dough, for which all that's needed is water and salt. The Turks did their baking from three in the morning, in a street buried beneath rubble on one side, kneading the dough behind the streetside serving hatch of a kebab shop that was sealed over with black plastic sheeting, kneading the dough to the rhythm of Black Sea rap music, then Igor and Elina would load the crates of flatbreads with their bulging brown scabs onto the truck and distribute them round the housing estates first thing in the morning. Igor drove, cursing and swearing at the roads for being like a tankodrome, with Elina asking 'Why though?' and keeping an eye out for any hungry Russian missile that might be approaching.

'They say half of them don't even explode,' his Valkyrie remarked. She was slight of form, for Igor something of a lady, and she was apt to describe herself as being 'compact'. She believed her strength to be all the greater for God's having compressed her into a mere 155 centimetres, in short a compression spring. If she'd been 30 centimetres taller, she might have walked the catwalk in Odessa, though her long limbs would have been torpid, sluggish even.

'That means that every second one *will* explode,' Igor said, smirking, and tried to get the wipers to remove a bit of polythene that had landed on their windscreen at the last crossroads.

'So like that glass then.'

He glanced at her, puzzled.

'You don't know? You really are a bit green still. If you've got a glass with some water in it, for some people it's half-empty and for others half-full.'

'Meaning what, then?'

'Meaning that Russian missiles are either half-successful or half-unsuccessful, it all depends on your nature.'

'If everything depended on my nature, then right now I'd be shagging our biology teacher,' Igor observed as he steered cautiously round a burnt-out car in the middle of the road.

Elina looked through the window to check the car was unoccupied and muttered under her breath: 'Oh my God.'

Before long, the development on the eastern side of the city loomed into view. The white trunks of birch trees stood out against the smoke-blackened facades and there was one block that you could see right through: the glass in the windows of the one surviving wall had been shattered, the window frames burnt away, leaving just savage holes in the wall sections to be invaded implacably by the blue of the sky. A group of people stood trying to warm their hands beside a fire outside the main entrance, and within sight of them two kids in gaily coloured anoraks were having a high old time on a swing, standing up on it. Igor and Elina hopped out of the truck and took out a crate.

Last time they'd had a bit of a row at this stage. Elina maintained the flatbreads should be free. But Igor and the Turks had struck their own bargain, half for them, half for him, they were in it fifty-fifty, not to put too fine a point on it. He'd even offered his good lady Samaritan half of his half, but she'd just given him an earful. So now the method was that she handed out the lavash like some saint in a funk, then he had to bum the shekels out of them like a complete scrounger.

He knew a lot of them by sight, from the shops, the bus, from this very place. He'd grown up here, and even a week before he'd been living here with his mother and kid sister. Then came the first round of shelling, the first night that they'd crawled into the bathroom, because a bathroom has no windows, his mother had held his kid sister in her arms and he'd tried to find out what the fuck was going on. On the fourth day, at two in the morning, the shock wave from an explosion right outside their building knocked out the windows in both rooms. Even before that he'd covered them in strips of sticky tape as a precaution against splinters—for once it proved useful to have had a green brain for a father. Nothing happened to them and the following day they'd moved to the city centre instead, to the hotel where his mother worked and which now served as a place of refuge. Igor was quite at one with their move, having in his mind all too clear an image of the Russian soldier, a dimwit, a kid who'd found himself at war before any bird had given him his first blow-job and hadn't noticed that this wasn't just another online shoot-out. A nine-storey high-rise with three entrances was just asking for it, so big and defenceless you couldn't miss it with even the stupidest bomb in the world.

'Your biology teacher, that's just some cliché, right?' Elina remarked as they headed for their next stop. She thought the situation demanded they keep up an illusion of everyday life and chat about all and sundry. 'Why not the history teacher?'

'Old Anton? I ain't that desperate!'

'So another cliché: biology teachers are always young lasses straight out of college, while history's taught by old fogeys who've seen life.'

Igor shrugged. 'True, now and again Anton would go on a bit about how he'd served in Afghanistan.'

'Are you at the engineering college?'

Igor nodded. The Azovstal Iron and Steel Works split the city into its eastern and western halves. To the south it was bordered by the Sea of Azov, to the north by a main highway. Rusting blast furnaces, endless gantry crane rails, railway tracks, suspension bridges and walkways, kilometres of pipelines and an endless labyrinth of underground passages: the iron heart of Mariupol. For one thing though, no one knew for sure just what its chimneys were belching out. She only had to enter the city from outside, spend a week somewhere else and Elina could smell those toxic fumes at once. On the buses everybody kept coughing up phlegm like during the flu season, little kids' skin turned yellow, and if anyone in Mariupol painted the front of their house, within the year it got fouled up beneath a veneer of greasy ash so thick you could draw dirty pictures in it.

'And you?' he asked. 'What were you doing before all this?'

She was surprised he was showing any interest in her; this was perhaps the first time this lad with close-cropped hair, big eyes and ears that stood out from his head had asked her something. 'Only a fortnight ago I was still at work in my own veterinary practice.'

'My kid sister's got a hamster. Stupidest creature I've ever seen.'

'I grew up with animals. Grandad had some stables. I had no option. For a time it even looked as if I was to become a jockey.'

Igor turned off towards a bakery that was closed and in front of which another mound of human jelly was shaking. This time he left the distribution of flatbreads to Elina even though it meant he wouldn't make a penny from this crate. They were quite near their flat and he'd promised his sister to pick up her diary, which she'd left there. And then for his mother, no joking, the pack of sanitary towels from the cupboard under the sink, 'cause they weren't to be had now for love or money.

*

He first spotted the sexpot by the aquarium inside the Hotel Europa. He'd got back from their rounds completely knackered and, above all, late, because on their way back a shell had shot over their heads and exploded barely a hundred metres away. They'd been the first on the scene and found in the flat that took the hit a mother in shock and a child soaked in blood. They'd loaded them onto the back of the pick-up like into an ambulance and Igor had tried to use his radio to find where the nearest working hospital was. As they crossed the hotel car park it dawned on him for the first time that hereabouts things could easily turn out badly for him as well. In those ten days he'd lost count of the number of corpses he'd already seen, but even so he hadn't had the slightest inkling that that corpse over there on the grass or the one in that car or the one under that bench could have been him. Death had nothing to do with him, any more than rabbit plague did, though for rabbits it's certainly no joke. But after ten days he'd had his basinful. There was no running water, so he stank like an old pine marten, he might as well

109

have tried sticking his fingers in all his various sockets, nothing else worked, and without any signal he'd lost his mates from his vocational school, all those birds on TikTok and the entire rest of the internet. Hmm, and now it looked as if even hospitals weren't functioning—he was no expert, but he was pretty sure it wasn't normal for patients to snuff it wired up to instruments that weren't switched on.

So this was the stuff going round inside his head as he entered the wreckage of the hotel lobby. And the girl was still standing there, gawping at it, gawping into the aquarium, that stupid fish-world, as if nothing else existed. She looked totally out of it, but he was in no mood to see what was wrong with her, 'cause there was plenty wrong with everyone right then, and he headed straight for the side staircase, which was still where it should be, unlike the main one.

The hotel had also taken a direct hit, otherwise they wouldn't have dared to be here: there'd come a moment when it was clear that buildings that had already been struck were safer, with Russian helicopters overhead on the hunt for new targets. In the night, they—he, his mother, kid sister and others—would hunker down in the basement, but by day they'd look for a bit of privacy in one of the hotel rooms on the first floor. It was there that Igor found the two of them, amid the luxury of velvet wallpaper and sculpted bedside tables that was well beyond their normal experience.

'But you haven't read it, have you?' Masha was anxious to know when he handed her the dust-covered diary with a unicorn on the cover. In the course of the day their mother had found time to wind Masha's hair into nine blonde plaits that had sucked in every last strand so that Masha now looked like a bald-headed Medusa with long snakelets.

'You mean the bit where you write about that boy?'

'You dummy!'

'Everything all right?' his mother asked, placing a hand on his forehead.

He jerked back, he never liked it when she touched him. 'Perfect,' he said with deliberate irony. 'Here as well?'

'Pretty much. Looks as if we've got new neighbours,' she said, pointing at the wall, from behind which came noises like someone having fun with a rotary sander. 'Do you want a bite to eat? Though we don't have any meat.'

'That rhymes!' Masha squealed. 'Mummy's a poet and she doesn't know it!' Then she went on repeating endless variants on the theme: 'Bite to eat? Any meat. Smelly feet . . .'

'Did you know your dad an' I once spent a night 'ere?' his mother began, pushing the pan across to him. 'Not summat we could ever afford in 't normal way o' things. But we was newly married an' I'd got together wi' a friend who were on reception and another who were a chambermaid, your dad came to pick me up an' I surprised 'im.'

Igor gulped down the mash, which had gone cold. His mother had been a waitress in the restaurant at the Europa for as long as he could remember. And that was quite something, because mostly the guy who ran it would keep replacing the staff with younger elements to ensure a steady flow of pretty faces and lissom bodies, but he'd kept her on. Probably to have someone to do all the work while the rest were having it away in the office, as Igor imagined. Now it suited them very well indeed, because they knew the place like the back of their hands.

'It could even be that it were 'ere I got pregnant wi' you,' she added.

'For God's sake, Mum . . .'

Over the last three years this was about the fifteenth place where he'd been conceived. Igor had never quite got it, but his mother was totally obsessed with the idea. It had started during a military operation eight years before, the army was trying to dislodge the separatists and had actually gained control of the city except somewhere along the line his father had lost his self-control. It hadn't been a heroic death, but it had come about 'in a heroic context', as his commanding officer had put it, and so he'd been pronounced a hero. What was odder was that his mother even believed it. Probably because she'd been pregnant with Masha at the time and told herself that if the poor kid was to grow up fatherless, she could at least be the posthumous child of a hero.

'I tell you,' said Igor as he licked the pan clean, 'it's all goin' from bad to worse. You really ought to grab Masha an' go.'

'And where to, if you don't mind me askin'? Anyway, I couldn't leave you here.'

'Don't matter where. Away from 'ere. Even to Russia if that's all that's left. You don't know what things are like further away.'

'Your old mum knows very well what's goin' on.'

Igor glanced at her impatiently. 'Nobody knows! We don' even know if things are lookin' the same in Kharkiv and Kyiv. Suppose out there the army's already surrendered an' the fightin' 'ere's only 'cause of the steelworkers.'

'Even if I did want to go, there's no way.'

'Not yet. But they'll send some buses in. You 'ave to be ready. Think about 'er,' said Igor with a nod towards the bathroom, where Masha had locked herself in to add some stuff to her diary.

As they made their way down to the basement about an hour later, the girl was still standing in the hotel lobby, gawping into the aquarium as if she wanted to stare it out of existence. The fish tank itself still glimmered among the overturned tables and chairs. The girl was wearing a dark suede jacket with squiggles all over it, some shiny and some black, and she was made up with cat eyes. She looked totally unaware of any war going on, as if she'd simply come into town because it was Friday evening. Except it probably wasn't even Friday.

'Shubunkins,' she said as they were passing.

His mother smiled politely in her direction as if she were some kind of loony and walked on past, but Masha couldn't resist and stopped beside her.

'They're all called just goldfish as well,' the girl said. 'Isn't that orangey veiltail a beauty? With its fins coming out like flames, see?'

Masha looked at the fish and then, slightly uncertain of herself, at Igor.

'Or that one, it's a peacock goldfish, quite something, isn't it?' the girl said, pointing a blue-varnished finger nail at another of the fish. 'Do you know why they're called that?'

Masha shook her head.

'Because their tailfins spread out like a peacock's. Have you ever seen a peacock?'

'And this one?' asked Masha, without answering the question and pointing to another fish with long, dark-purple fins that looked lacerated.

'That's a Siamese fighting fish,' the girl said. 'You can never have more than one male in the same tank, otherwise they fight to the kill. But it's only their own kind that bothers them, they treat all other fish quite naturally. Even if the other fish nibble at those long fins they have! They just leave them alone. They only attack any that look like themselves. Just like humans.'

Igor took a few steps towards Masha and took her by the hand, playing safe. Couldn't the girl see the stupid fish were all floating belly-up?

'They really are beautiful, aren't they?' the girl said. 'And with that gold one there as well you can make a wish. So, go for it.'

'Can I wish for anything at all?' Masha wanted to be sure.

'Yes, but only one, right now we can't afford any kind of wastage.'

Igor didn't know whether the girl really was far gone, or what the hell was going on. Was she completely nuts? People

114

were forever telling him he was no genius, but at least he'd got all his marbles.

'But all those fish are dead,' he said at last.

The girl shot him a pitying glance like he was some retard.

'Maybe it's been a long time since anyone changed their water . . . But more likely it's just got a bit too cold in here. They're tropical fish and if the aquarium drops below twenty they start to lose their colour, slip into rigour, stop moving and in the end they simply die. Like humans.'

The following day the Turks ran out of flour. Igor parked next to a fallen tree that looked as if it had been gnawed through by a beaver, though no one in Mariupol had ever seen a beaver. From down in the basement up to street level came, as usual, the thud of Black Sea rap issuing from packing cases attached to a diesel generator, interspersed with the wailing of sirens. Sirens? They might enjoy that luxury in Ivano-Frankivsk or Lviv, but in Mariupol there'd been no sirens to go wailing for a long time now. There were only three crates of lavash anyway, instead of fifteen, so the Turks had begun baking using emergency supplies from the militia. And melting some of the snow that had landed on the city during the night to bring at least some relief to people's wounds.

For Igor that meant two things. For one, he literally couldn't sell lavash any more 'cause his line of business had been nationalized after a fashion. And for another, he'd have to go and get a sack of flour from the army warehouse now and again, and that was some way off. Under normal circumstances that wouldn't be a problem, except now the streets were adorned with ever more immobilized wrecks or covered in rubble, there were heaps of rubbish everywhere or they'd been bombed to smithereens, plain and simple.

But it was those wrecks that gave Igor a new idea. Most of the burnt-out cars were just skeletons, but here and there the odd useful bit could still be dismantled from what was otherwise a write-off. In one side street he'd raised a bonnet and found that the engine beneath had survived unscathed, only the rubber bits having been frizzled away and any aluminium melted. There was this guy on the estate who worked at a body shop and might be glad enough of the odd pointer to some abandoned Beemer or Audi to slip him something.

Once more they were driving through the estate, but this time the Valkyrie in the front passenger seat was oddly taciturn. Usually, she rabbited on like some woman on a mission, asking him about everything under the sun and dragging out of him even stuff he'd never have thought he'd ever yield up to her. But not this time. This time she just let her gaze wander over the utter horror of it all. He parked in the usual place, and since there was nothing in it for him anymore, she could get on with it and dish out the flatbreads by herself while he went in search of the guy from the body shop.

He found him squatting outside the entrance, where only a month back, they'd chainsmoked together. But somehow Sasha wasn't his normal self either. He did listen to what Igor had to say, nodding from time to time, but insisted this wasn't a good time for business. Igor knew that too, but the war wasn't going to last forever—sooner or later garages were going to be overwhelmed, someone was going to have to mend all those old crocks, right? To which Sasha said he honestly had no idea how he'd get the wrecks off the road right now and refused to discuss the matter further.

'We've basically 'ad it 'ere,' he declared.

Only now did Igor take a proper look around. Someone had taken the children's playground across the road, where once he'd played himself, and buried it underground. And in the middle of the pit, besides the twisted climbing frames and the melted slide, there was also a body wrapped in a blanket. It came back to him that drunks would sometimes be found sleeping in playgrounds, like the guy he remembered from when he was quite small and who he'd surprised one Sunday morning: he'd spent Saturday night boozing, got as far as his front door, but then his old lady had refused to let him in. But this body here showed every sign of being frozen, with snow clinging to the folds of the blanket and to his greasy black hair.

Igor swore, Sasha offered him a fag and lit up himself. 'Why the hell don't they bury the poor bugger given 'e's already in that hole?' Igor ranted.

'Ground frozen that 'ard's almost impossible to dig,' Sasha drew on his fag and started coughing. 'So since the bomb's left an 'ole that big, we can shove more of 'em into it. Them as 'ave been kept in laundries an' pram rooms up to now.'

'What?'

117

'Before that we put 'em in the cellars, but now we need them for ourselves. You've no idea what's been goin' on 'ere of a night recently.'

"Ow many . . . is there?'

'Not rightly sure. They'll be bringing 'em out shortly, then you'll see. This one were nearest, so 'e's keepin' a spot for the others. 'Ere they come now,' said Sasha, pointing.

Igor saw two guys carrying a third between them, wrapped in a rug that was too narrow and with his legs poking out. They got as far as the crater, where they gently slid him in. Igor was frightened the runner would unfold, but the guys had taken care of that and bound it round with carpet tape.

Sasha stubbed his fag out on the concrete and said: 'D'you mind givin' us a hand since you're 'ere?'

Igor stared back at him with question marks in his eyes.

'My grandad,' said Sasha with a shrug. 'We're on 't second floor. But you know that already. 'Cept this time it'll be wi'out 't lift.'

They clambered up and along the corridors and entered the small high-rise flat. Igor had a vague recollection that Sasha lived with just his grandparents, but couldn't remember why anymore. A wind was blowing through the flat, Sasha led him into the bedroom, where his grandmother was sitting on the wrinkled white bedspread, staring at her late husband beside her. It looked as if someone had done a good job, the old man really did look like a dead person, a proper dead person: he had no visible injuries, was dressed in a suit and a fittingly vague expression had settled on his face.

The old woman rose without a word. Sasha showed Igor that they'd got it all thought out: they'd wrap his grandad in the very bedspread on which he was lying.

As they carried him out he didn't weigh much. Igor had noticed before that in old age people chucked the sandbags from their hot-air balloon, relieving the weight a bit.

Now they were outside the front of the house, the pit in the playground was surrounded by people on all sides, among them Elina, who stood aside for them as they made to deposit the old man with the others. Two guys offered to check the buildings nearby, where they did find another one nobody had laid claim to.

There was no priest to be had, but Elina suggested that, if nobody objected, she could at least recite a prayer. One old boy muttered that any prayer should be said by a man, but none of the men present seemed to remember one, so that settled it.

The Valkyrie adjusted her rifle sling, everyone fell silent and she began, slowly: 'Lord Jesus Christ, Son of God, Thy holy will be done in all things.'

Igor stared hard at the ground.

'May God arise, may His enemies be scattered and may those who hate God flee before Him, as smoke is blown away so shall they be blown away. As wax melts before fire, so let demons perish from the face of those who love God.'

A handful of flowers fell onto the corpses, including a few of the first snowdrops that, as any other spring, would spring up right there among the tower blocks.

'Glory to Thee, O God. Lord God, give succour now to us who are powerless. Amen.'

*

Igor found it odd how quickly people could get used to certain things. Though perhaps not quite, but they do adapt, as that biology teacher of theirs used to say when talking about evolution. Perhaps one day he himself would evolve into a new species, something clever and hardy. For the time being, though, he thought there'd been quite enough for one day. He'd not slept much and seen rather more than he cared to. But now it wasn't even midday and Elina had just said there was still something she had to deal with. Dealing with something else was the last thing he felt like, all he wanted was to shove his head under a pillow and wake up in the summer; what would summer bring? But Elina seemed disinclined to discuss the matter.

'What's this about?' he asked once they were back inside the battered white pick-up.

'Horses.'

'What 'orses?'

'My horses!' It wasn't obvious if she'd bounced off her seat because he'd just hit a pothole, or if that compressed spring inside her had been released. He'd seen that a couple of times already, whenever she got het up over something, she'd bounce up and down. 'I told you I've got some horses, didn't I?'

'You said yer grandad 'ad some stables when you was little.'

'Well Grandad's no longer with us, but the stables are. In Staryi Krym.'

'So what?'

'It's also being shelled now. I have to take care of them.'

'You can take the car,' was the best offer he could make her there and then.

'I don't have a licence.'

'Nor do I. And no one gives a fuck about that right now.'

'The point is I don't know how to drive.'

'Tough luck then,' Igor concluded. 'Horses, now, holy shit!' He looked at her in disbelief.

But in the very next instant he understood that the discussion was over, but with a different outcome. Not that he was gazing down its barrel, but his Valkyrie had just shifted her rifle slightly on her lap so that now it was sort of aiming at him.

'I'll navigate,' she said by way of encouragement.

Staryi Krym lies at the very edge of Mariupol, actually just beyond. Igor had taken the trouble a few times to visit its huge cemetery, because he had relatives buried there, but right now he hadn't the slightest desire to pay them a visit, let alone join them. Not even Elina knew exactly where the front line was. But probably not that far away, with shells now flying about her stables.

They came to a halt behind the queue of cars held at a road-block and purely from boredom Igor asked: "Ow come it never worked out?'

'What?'

'You told me last time as you wanted to be a jockey, right?'

'Oh, that. It's true, I was seventeen at the time and—that's how old you are, isn't it?'

'An' I'll be gettin' given a rifle before long, then I won"ave to listen to you.'

'And you'll pay the price accordingly,' she smirked. 'It was the run-up to my first big race. But then during training Atlantis—that was my horse's name—balked at one jump. At the last minute he tried to swerve, but lost his footing in the mud. I was flung to the ground and he landed on top of me. He was only there for a second, but a horse can weigh as much as half a ton. Crushed thigh, three broken vertebrae, twelve months in a corset. The doctor said I should prepare for a lifetime in a wheelchair. But I pulled through somehow, except for this leg and few other bits and pieces.'

'An' there was me thinkin' as 'ow you'd got that limp fightin',' he snorted.

'Life itself is a fight.'

'Why would any woman wear camo? Don' you 'ave no kids?'

'You really are dim. Anyway, because of that fall I can't have children. My children are my horses. That's why we're going there.'

Igor nodded in resignation, thought a while, then asked: 'So what are we gonna do wi''em?'

'I've spent the entire morning trying to figure something out.'

'Don' you be thinkin' that . . .' The prospect of taking a horse somewhere horrified him. And how.

'The only solution is to let them go.'

'Let 'em go?'

'Yes, let them go. There's no way I can get them to safety. I can't bring them here, the explosions would drive them crazy. And at the stables they'll burn to death sooner or later, or be killed by shell fragments. I have to hope they'll be able to manage on their own.'

Goodness knows why, but that made quite an impression on Igor. Originally he'd meant to say how many people could feast on half a ton of horseflesh, but then thought better of it.

'It'll be spring soon,' Elina added as if needing to convince herself, 'maybe they really will cope. Though I'd rather leap into Western's saddle and charge off to give some Russian tank a kick up the arse. Seeing as how those shitbags are laying siege to us like in the Middle Ages.'

When their turn came, the home guard militiaman tried to explain to Elina that the road to Staryi Krym was anything but safe. The enemy, he jested, was even shelling the cemetery so he could add a few more corpses to his tally. Then he turned serious again and showed her on a map everywhere where the Russians were—showed her they were everywhere.

123

Igor went back to the car. He tried putting the radio on but lately all you heard on any frequency was rustling, booming and whistling noises. He twiddled all the pre-settings before switching to search, but all he got was crackling. As if Mariupol had vanished from the face of the earth down to the bottom of the Mariana Trench. Though probably all you'd get there would be a several-kilometres-deep silence.

The soldiers let them through at their own risk. The frozen, deeply rutted roadway led between the two sections of the cemetery, and the stables lay just beyond, where at that moment it just happened to be all quiet. They drove up to an old building with crumbling plaster and Igor parked the car. Elina opened her door and hadn't even started to get out when a dog's head appeared on her lap.

'We're taking this fellow back with us,' she said.

They ran quickly inside and the horses began to whinny. Elina opened the boxes and led them outside. Igor's eye fell on one horse, black as charcoal, don't they call them raven-black? He knew the expression from the fairy tale he used to read to Masha before it got swallowed up by his iPad, and they fished it out again of late after the iPad died. In it, a raven-black stallion goes charging with its rider through a forest full of goblins, and the bit Masha liked best was when the horse is leaping over a precipice and finds it can fly, because it's descended from Pegasus.

Igor approached the horse cautiously and patted it on its shiny shoulder.

'That's Western,' said Elina. 'He's the one I ride these days.'

The horses were probably expecting Elina to saddle them up, but instead she even removed their stable collars. And then she bade farewell to each of them in turn: she laid her head against each of theirs and for just a few seconds stood there with her forehead resting just above their muzzles. She finally made a huge sign of the cross over each long head, took a step back and began firing into the air.

*

When, later that day, they finally got back to the hotel, the sexpot was back in the lobby. He hadn't seen her for some time, but now she was leaning against one of the tables, half sitting on it, and down between her legs a cat was lying in wait. Out of a polythene bag the girl took another dead aquarium fish, held it by the tailfin and dangled it in the air. The cat crouched back, briefly hypnotizing the fish and then smashed every high jump record in the book. The fish was a veiltail, the one with blazing fins, a goldfish, she mumbled something, the cat sprang, snapped the fish between its teeth, landed on all fours and carried it off happily under a table at the back.

Igor watched the girl from a distance and then went closer up to the aquarium. It had gone dark, the battery supplying the LEDs had died, or someone had dumped it in the water. Even so he could tell there were no fish left in it, living or dead, and the water level had also gone down as people had begun scooping it out into pots. Even this supply was obviously not going to last long, though people had agreed among themselves that no one would take more than two litres a day. His mother couldn't get over it, never having had such kindly neighbours: the women looked after each other's kids, the menfolk went out breaking branches off trees so there was something to cook on, and in the evenings they'd all gather over a shared meal.

The sole topic of conversation was how to get out of the town. Every day was supposed to see the arrival of Red Cross buses, except they never showed up. People came back home frozen to the marrow, gradually realizing that if they wanted to get away, they had to fix it for themselves. One evening, one guy piled all his family into an ancient Zhiguli, but he hadn't got a kilometre beyond the town when they were shot at. Shrapnel ripped the bodywork open like a can of beans, the window glass shattered and the main thing was that his wife got hit several times. Now she was lying with her head bandaged up in what had been the vegetable store behind the hotel kitchens, raving on the mattress that had previously been rolled up on the car's roof.

'I'm not sure, not sure . . . ,' said the girl when the cat came back for more. 'This fish is slightly poisonous.'

By now Igor was totally puzzled. She still had those striking black lines around her eyes, and now she'd daubed her lips as well. In her leather jacket and fishnet tights she looked quite sexy, pity she's so bonkers. Or maybe it don't matter? He were pretty sure it wouldn't matter to them Russian scumbags.

'So better not let it 'ave the fish, right?' he shouted across to her.

'Aha, you're still here. Thing is, she's still hungry.'

'But you just said the bloody fish is poisonous.'

The girl grinned. 'That's the way of the world: you want a thing and it's the one thing that'll kill you.'

He's spent the day driving round a bombed-out town and now this? He stepped up nice and close to her to show who's boss hereabouts and snatched the fish from her. As he did so, something drove into his hand. 'Bloody 'ell!'

'Careful now, lionfish have got spines,' the girl said as she patted him on the cheek.

'Ow, fuck!' Igor wailed, gripping the affected hand with the other. It hurt like hell. It wasn't just that he'd pricked himself, it felt as if his whole hand could drop off any second.

'I reckon she's brighter than you and will leave the spines well alone,' the girl opined as she watched the cat cautiously inspecting the fish where it lay on the ground. 'They contain quite nasty venom. Your hand'll start to swell and you won't be able to move it for a while,' she said, taking his hand in hers as if about to tell him his fortune. 'You might have a little trouble breathing at night. But you're unlikely to die. Though if you do, I'll testify you died on the battlefield, just like in your old man's case.'

'My old man?' He eased his sore hand from her grip. It hurt as much as if he were holding a tin mug full of piping-hot tea. But he was also aware of getting heated in other ways. She was still half-standing, half-sitting on the edge of the table, directly opposite him, her legs in those fishnet tights slightly apart the way she'd left a space for the cat.

127

'Well?' She prodded his shoulder. 'D'you wanna kiss me? I'd think twice about it if I were you.'

The tart was trying to provoke him.

'No, no, I'm not playin' games with you.' She turned away as he tried to kiss her. 'You'd better go to your mum—you got back late today, she's bound to be worried stiff whether you're safe.'

He grabbed her by the chin and forced her face back towards him. He stared into her eyes as if spitting in them, but she didn't even flinch. 'Just you wait,' he said, let go of her and staggered off with his burning hand up to the first floor.

He managed to fall asleep, but it wasn't long before Masha woke him for supper. Within the hotel, eating together had become a ritual. They pushed a number of tables together in the basement, covered them in white tablecloths and decorated them with candles. Under normal circumstances, the fancy crockery was meant to impress the hotel's posher clients, but now they were doling out potato fritters onto it. At the table, Igor enjoyed a degree of respect because he could tell them how things were looking in other parts of the city as well as stuff he'd got from the soldiers. And similarly they hung onto every word uttered by one girl who, for her part, knew where to go to catch a mobile-phone signal, and after a day's wait she really had managed to download some bits of news. So they learned that even as peace talks were going on the bastards were shelling the evacuation corridor.

They understood that the whole world was watching them, understood that the whole world was just watching. They opened the last few bottles of fizz from the hotel's stock and watched as the candles burnt down.

Igor tossed and turned his way through the night, unable to fall asleep. His injured hand was poking out from the mattress, while Masha lay across his other arm, breathing quietly and huddled up to him. He'd lost all feeling in that arm but had a dull twitching sensation in his bad hand: such a tiny spine, an' the damn' fish 'ad been dead for days!

He closed his eyes and tried counting slowly to a hundred. The explosions in the distance sounded like fireworks on New Year's Eve. As recently as two months ago the area around the Drama Theatre had been a blaze of light, the giant Christmas tree outside the entrance had pulsed with flashing lights, and away from the building into the park led four flickering tunnels which Masha had walked up and down spellbound.

When he and Elina had passed that way today, they saw someone writing on the paving in letters 10 metres tall the word ДЕТИ – Children.

Also, two months back, he and a bunch of his mates had been knocking about on the very shore from which they were now being bombarded. He also had a vision of part of that New Year's night: Azovstal had been belching out orange clouds, but the sea didn't smell so bad in winter and they'd got smashed on vodka. Not in the port, but next to the huge mountain of slag that seems to grow right out of the sea, just like elsewhere actual mountains rear up from the coast. It was there that they'd bet the next bottle on who'd be the first to shag Halina, the biology teacher. Igor swore blind he'd done it that summer, having chatted her up as she was sunbathing on the beach; first she'd played hard to get, but then she'd rolled over onto her back. Bollocks, his mates had protested and they'd been right, but he'd been right too, because that was exactly how he'd imagined it whenever he jerked himself off in the bathroom at home. How long was it now since he'd last done that? Fuckin' war!

Masha stirred, grabbed his arm in her sleep and wound herself round him like a liana. Masha . . . Before the meal she'd shown him the pictures she'd drawn during the day. Not on paper, but on the basement walls, like in some primaeval cave. She and the other kids had spent the day drawing and now she was parading this infantile feed before him: the boys had posted the tanks with giant guns, the helicopters and aircraft that were going to chase the bloody Russians back beyond the Urals, the girls much the same, plus some lost pets.

In a corner Masha had drawn him and herself, holding hands across the right angle as if they might be able to hide in that very corner. 'Masha, Mashenka . . .' He took a deep breath but was unable to continue, then said something he hadn't meant to: he just said he'd seen real live horses today. She'd looked at him open-mouthed and he had to promise that next time he went to see them he'd take her with him.

In the gloom of the night he saw her eyes twitching beneath her lids and he envied her being able to sleep amid the din. He could hear her breathing and wished he could hide in it like in a little boat carried along on the waves, but it wouldn't come.

He stuck plugs in his ears, but that didn't help either. After another hour spent vainly trying to drop off, he carefully rolled over and started discreetly wanking off—in a room where another thirty people were sleeping, or not. He had to use his left hand, because the other had been put out of action by that spiteful lionfish and could, at best, hold his hankie. He closed his eyelids tight, pulled down Halina's bikini top and, without even knowing how, started stroking the bird in the fishnet tights between her legs.

*

After the not quite three weeks since the war began the lavash flatbreads had definitely run out. The last time Igor went to pick some up—now baked more from dust and ashes than flour—it was no longer Black Sea rap coming from the kebab shop, but voices raised in anger. The Turks were going at it so furiously that they didn't even hear him hammering at the door, so he had to get back in the car and use his horn. They did come to the door but carried on arguing as if he wasn't even there, he couldn't understand a word, but it was plain that the air was turning blue with the foulest of profanities. After ten minutes they calmed down a bit and the one who had a slight grasp of surzhyk, the local Russo-Ukrainian patois, explained the gravity of the situation to him—they'd learned that those filthy soddin' Greeks had gone and got eighty-two people out of the city. 'Can you credit it?' the Turk flared up again. 'Did the Greeks ever do any good by anyone? An' they're the first to get away, the arseholes!'

Igor drove round to check that neither the home guard nor the army had any flour left. Returning along the shattered streets he suddenly had no idea what to do next. Anyone able to was trying to get away.

Even those Turks were hoping that some bigwig back home would wake up, seeing as how Greek diplomacy had given them a right kick in the pants. He was thoroughly browned off, totally fed up. There were nights when bombs fell every ten minutes and days when artillery fire didn't let up for ten hours on end. He repeatedly told his mother she had to be prepared—if some-one from the home guard came with a message that the buses had got through, she wasn't to hesitate for a single second. A week before he'd packed Masha's little knapsack and written along her arm all conceivable data and contacts in case she happened to get lost.

One part of him wanted nothing more than to get on that bus with the rest, but the other him was being held back by something. It wasn't over yet.

He spent the next two days at the hotel, but that was the worst. Only now did he understand how lucky he'd been to be able to move about on the outside. At least he'd seen what was going on and not been quaking like a mouse in a hole that could be left buried underground at any moment. At the hotel there was no avoiding his mother or all those others who were also getting on his nerves by this stage. His buggered hand still hurt and during the day he was hungry because the only mealtime was in the evening, and there wasn't much of it anyway. Everything had turned to shit.

His spirits rose slightly next day when Elina showed up. She even had with her that tyke they'd brought from the stables. Her building had now also taken a hit and she was thankful she'd got away unscathed.

After they stopped doing their lavash rounds, she'd been taking turns at roadblocks. The day before, she'd got caught up in a gun battle and from the way she talked, or rather didn't talk, about it, Igor gathered she'd reached her limit. Maybe she'd bumped someone off, or maybe she'd had a narrow squeak herself, from her bewildered silence you couldn't tell.

Now they were stood together in a small stockroom that had become a smoking room, because it had a tiny window just below the ceiling, wondering what to do next. Masha was there with them, bending down now and again to tickle the dog rolling about at her feet like it was stoned, and it stank to high heaven, but then who didn't?

'Ain't it occurred to you to do a runner?' Igor queried.

Elina let out a sigh. 'A couple of days ago, they say, a few dozen cars managed to get through. And yesterday there were several thousand,' she said. 'But it really is full-blooded Russian roulette. They let one car go, then start shooting at the next one. One day a whole convoy gets through, the next day they do a convoyoscopy on the lot. Depends what mood you catch them in. Or what state they're in.'

Igor hadn't the foggiest what colonoscopy meant, let alone her convoyoscopy, but it couldn't be anything nice if it were something Russians did to people. He took a long drag then rested his outstretched arm, fag in hand, on the wall close to the little window. 'She 'as to leave,' he said, pointing its orange tip at Masha. 'But I'd put more trust in buses, the bastards can't shoot up an entire humanitarian convoy.'

'But they might not let the buses come anywhere near. Or they could force the drivers to change course and head into Russia.'

'My problem is that our ma wants us all to scarper together. Keeps goin' on about she ain't goin' nowhere wi'out me.'

'That's because you're at a blooming awkward age,' she opined, tapping her fag ash onto her forearm—she didn't know how to smoke, having only just started, and she was so tiny that she couldn't reach anywhere near the window. 'If you fancied giving it a go, I've had a tip about one guy who ferries people out. He's got a Volga and knows a safe route.'

'That won't come cheap now, eh?'

'But you've made a bit of cash, haven't you?' she said with a grin.

'Remember 'ow we went to let your 'orses go? It looked okay out there as well . . .'

'Horses?' Masha piped up. 'I want to go on a horse!'

'That makes two of us,' Elina interjected, turning again to Igor. 'We were probably just lucky. Look, I shan't hold it against you if you pack up and disappear. If you're so minded, just go. Anyone will understand. And that guy with the Volga, all he asks for is the cost of petrol, otherwise he's doing it because he believes it's the right thing to do.'

'An' would you come wi' us?'

Elina looked at him. 'Honest, I won't hold it against you. But I've also been thinking: as long as we're here with a car that still works, we oughtn't to be sitting around on our backsides. It's occurred to me we could be something like an ambulance. You as driver and me as, erm . . .'

'A vet?'

'That'll do. A vet specializing in humans.'

'A vet specializing in humans?'

She explained that that made more sense than it might sound: in war there's lots of heavy bleeding to be stopped, wounds to be stitched up, and at her practice she'd had plenty of experience of both. 'Human tissue isn't that special,' she said, stubbing her cigarette out on the wall.

'No? An' I thought you was a Christian . . .'

'Look here, you!' She flicked her dog-end at him. 'You're not as green as you're cabbage-looking.'

Not that he'd ever wanted to be an ambulance driver. But he did know it'd be better than hanging about in the hotel. All he insisted on was being given a rifle at last. Who, for shit's sake, cares about a couple o' months this way or that? In two months it might be all over. Or all over with him.

They needed some basic equipment at least. They went round several abandoned hospitals that hadn't been looted yet, or only a bit haphazardly. Elina was looking for disinfectants and needles and threads, Igor trying to lay hands on some distilled water. But water were a right bloody problem, there weren't none left anywhere. People collected it from puddles, put pans out and rammed plastic bottles up drainpipes whenever it started to rain.

It occurred to him they might try using water from the aquarium if they boiled it properly. No good for infants, sure, but better than nothing. It took some persuading, but Elina managed to arrange for them to scoop out five litres a day.

Now that people had started taking water from the aquarium for cooking purposes, its level had dropped to about a quarter. One old boy constantly suspected everybody of taking more than their due and insisted that each taker drew a line on the glass and signed it. Elina just couldn't believe it, but the old fusspot really had gone and got hold of a marker pen, tied it to a bit of string and hung it up next to the aquarium. So now the side wall was prettily decked with lines and squiggles a centimetre apart.

It took them only a day to create their makeshift ambulance. All it now needed was the paint with which to add some red crosses to the battered white pick-up. Igor had got it all thought out: one cross on the bonnet, one on each side and an extra large one on the roof.

But this was right after the theatre had been bombed and Elina thumped him in the chest: 'You still don't get it, do you? It's not a good idea to offer them marked targets.'

*

Normally around mid-March the football season would begin. Igor played for the juniors, left back, cruising up and down the sideline. And now again he was being a defender of sorts, also keeping to a line, to be precise the centre line, because now that was just about the only way to drive along a road, unless you were in an armoured car. He failed to spot one large hole full of rubbish, yanked his wheel in the nick of time, his tyres screeching like at some tuning meetup. The pick-up tilted precariously to one side before mercifully landing back on all four.

Nothing went quite as they'd imagined. The home guard sent them to the sites of explosions if anyone had reported them, but more often than not they pitched in wherever they happened to be, at random. Only now did Elina appreciate the full extent of the destruction, not of buildings, not of streets, that had been evident long before, but now she realized all the things that had stopped working. If you made contact with, above all, the army or the home guard, you could be misled into thinking there was still some kind of command structure, that certain specific decisions were still being made for some good reason. But in the field that no longer held good: the city had fallen apart.

Fifteen minutes ago they'd been sent to another site. The hit had been taken by a school, which till now had been serving as a shelter. The building was on fire, but the city's fire brigade was no longer operating. They had no idea how many people were inside the building or how to reach them. They sat in the car, parked a little way back, and stared at the collapsing building in case someone made their way out. No one did. And even if they had, Elina knew they weren't equipped to deal with burns. One last hospital was still working, but even there no new patients were being taken in.

Igor leant on his steering wheel and stared into the flames billowing from the windows. The night before he'd met that girl again. For dinner he'd tossed down a plateful of greasy cracked barley and meant to nab some time for himself. He ran into her in the hotel lobby again and was momentarily at a complete loss as to what on earth she was up to. She was leaning out over the aquarium in nothing but a black nightie, although it was only ten degrees at most, and in what was left of the water she was soaking her long black hair. Only when she straightened up and frothed some shampoo into it did it dawn on him that the wench was simply washing her hair. In that remnant of water. Which they'd all been so sparing with. She was standing with her back to him and rubbing in the shampoo, then she got a bucketful of water from the aquarium and headed for the toilets to rinse it out. He shot after her and caught up with her just as she arrived in front of the sink.

She saw him in the mirror and said: 'You know, this really is totally pointless.'

He was standing behind her and suddenly it was as if something inside him had given. Like a string snapping. She were right. Everything were totally pointless. He went back into the lobby and stopped in front of the aquarium in which all that was left after her clean-up was a couple of inches of water.

And suddenly he saw things clearly: this aquarium's like this gut-wrenched city, the aquarium *is* Mariupol. First them tropical

138

fish died, then 't light went out, there were gradually less an' less water, an' now there's almost nothing at all, just a bit o' sand on 't bottom an' imprints o' dried-out water-weed on 't glass. An' what's worst, the whole world's standin' outside the glass and gawpin' as death gets closer and closer. If someone tipped rat poison into 't last bit o' water to speed things up a bit, the world'd be outraged, but it definitely won't shit itself.

'Shall we go, then?' Elina wrenched him away. Even a week ago a burning school would have brought a few of the locals running, and you'd have been able to find out a thing or two. But that's also long past. Now they were all hunkered down somewhere and hoping the next shell or *grad* rocket would miss them.

Having received no further reports, they casually set off back to the city centre, in case they might be of use near the theatre. On the way they stopped by the odd body lying in the road, just on the off chance, but no, not a chance. On one hand Igor recognized a ladies' Apple Watch, but he was feeling so lousy that he let it be. Hell, he thought, he'd actually feel ashamed, so that's what war does to you.

They arrived at the theatre, where they were told that all rescue work had been suspended because the area was still under fire, just to make sure: if there were any survivors, rescuing them was not to be made easy.

Elina begged Igor to drive round the corner to the Church of the Intercession of the Mother of God, inside which she disappeared.

Outside it had begun to rain, sleet it was, as if not even water could make up its mind as to its true nature. Igor sat in the car pondering over that tiny compressed woman praying beneath that huge dome. What could she be actually doing? And as he tried to imagine it, without knowing the words of a single prayer in the world, as he tried to imagine it with huge dollops of wet snow landing on the windscreen, it came to him, almost like a flash of inspiration, that he really had to leave. That he simply must take Masha, Elina and his mother away from this horror, where the only thing left to do was die like a dog. He wanted to be a bit of a hero, but without snuffing it in the process.

'I was having similar ideas myself, inside the church,' Elina concurred with a nod, having returned to her seat in the car.

*

They went back to the hotel. Elina changed into her civilian clothes and within ten minutes they'd tossed all their stuff into the car. They said their goodbyes to the others and left them their weapons.

Passing through the lobby, Igor noted that the aquarium now contained not one drop of water. The sand on the bottom was still wet, but that was all. Something made him reach in, grab a handful of sand and pop it in his pocket. In some future life he could use it to make an hourglass.

'Twenty years,' his mother sighed as they drove out of the carpark. She'd sat in the back with Masha, Elina's dog curled up among their feet.

Igor tried the radio, but again all he got was hissing, crackling and rumbling, like a broadcast from Radio Inferno.

They set off in the direction of Staryi Krym.

Masha hadn't been outside for weeks, and now she was gazing out of the window open-mouthed. Again her head was decked with those thin little plaits, the snakelets of Medusa, and after a moment she burst into tears.

'Why'd you let 'er see it?' Igor hissed into the mirror.

But his mother was also peering out goggle-eyed. Inside the hotel they'd sensed what the city must look like outside, but no one can know until he sees a thing with his own eyes.

The roadblock before the turn off the highway towards Staryi Krym had disappeared. The burnt-out remains of military hardware hinted at how.

Igor took the turn.

They drove past the cemetery wall, the trees were dripping and the heavy drops splattered as they hit the windscreen. The wipers weren't making proper contact with the glass and just smudged everything, the smears obliterating the contours of everything around.

Elina first thought her eyes were playing up. Ahead of them on the road stood a number of Russian jeeps and next to them a guy on horseback, stripped to the waist. His man boobs had a slight droop and there was a huge cross dangling between them. He looked to be demonstrating his horsemanship to the soldiers in the jeeps, but he just happened to be taking a warming tipple.

'Oh, shit,' Igor said under his breath. When he'd promised to take Masha to see some horses one day, he hadn't imagined it like this.

'That's my Western,' Elina whispered in disbelief, the wipers having started doing their job properly.

Igor slowed down and hoped the Russians could see the white rags tied round the wing mirrors. And take them for what they were. Two soldiers got out of the nearest jeep. One took aim at the white pick-up and the other indicated where they were to pull up.

Igor pulled into the side and wound down the window.

'You, out!' the soldier ordered.

He did as ordered and they told him to strip. They were looking for any tattoo that would link him to the Azov battalion. All they found was a tattooed number nine, the number Igor wore on his shirt when playing for his grassroots football team.

The Cossack leapt off his horse and stood facing Igor. Elina sensed things weren't looking good: they were standing opposite each other, both stripped to the waist, Igor looking sideways as the other subjected him to a scornful scrutiny.

The soldiers ordered the women out of the car as well. Elina tried not to look at Western, but he recognized her anyway and whinnied. They took their run-down phones off them, tossed Elina's iPhone to the damned Cossack and trampled the rest underfoot.

Masha stood there with her hands together and looked furtively at the horse.

'You're under eighteen, you can't drive,' the soldier who'd been studying their papers said.

'I'll drive,' Elina responded.

The soldier glanced her way, quite narked that a woman should have spoken at all. 'Only back the way you came. Go home and be safe, here you'd get caught in the crossfire.'

The Cossack measured Igor one more time, hopped back up into his saddle and took a gulp of vodka. 'Scram, before I have you tied up between this horse and the jeep.'

Igor was just reaching for the door on the driver's side when the soldier roared: 'What did I say? You don't have a license, she has to drive.'

Without a word he and Elina changed places and slammed their doors behind them.

'Oh shit,' she said under her breath, 'I don't have a clue what to do.'

'You'll only go a little way,' said Igor as calmly as he could, though he was shaking violently, half with cold, half in anger. 'Push 't left-hand pedal down to 't floor an' I'll turn 't ignition an' put it in first gear. Right. Now ease yer foot up slow like an' gi' it some gas wi' t'other.'

'Gas? Where the hell's that?'

He was so shattered he suddenly couldn't think straight. He had to switch feet blindly. 'Over on 't far right. So, let's go. Slowly, pedals in opposite directions.'

The pick-up coughed, hopped and died. From behind them came the sound of a horselaugh. 'The midget woman's so small she can't even reach the accelerator!' the infernal Cossack roared.

'One more time.'

A nervous Masha took the dog in her arms.

Elina tried once more to release the clutch and press the accelerator. This time the car juddered forward.

'That'll 'ave to do,' said Igor and switched on the wipers so they could see at least something. 'Now step on 't clutch again an' I'll put it in second.'

'And what about the wheel?'

'Jus' keep it straight.'

It looked like the worst was behind them. But they hadn't gone twenty metres when Igor noticed in the mirror that the Cossack on his horse had set off after them. First he just followed them, but then he bellowed something, raised his rifle and took aim jerkily.

'More, third!'

Then came the first gunshot. At the next the glass spilled from the rear window, his mother screamed and Masha began to cry. Elina put her foot down to the floor and the engine let out a whine. Igor grabbed the wheel from the side and tried to keep the car on the road. From behind came several more shots.

'Fuck!' Igor started to zigzag.

But the Cossack behind them had given up. He lowered his rifle, hauled on Western's reins and slowly receded into the distance.

With the cemetery on either side and the road between straight as a die, they could only change places after the first bend. Only then could Igor take a quick look at the rear seats. His mother was in tears and clutching Masha, who was clutching the dog. Blood everywhere. He had to keep his eye on the road, but Elina was already trying to establish what had actually happened at the rear. The mother seemed all right, but either Masha or the dog was bleeding, the dog's hair all matted. Then Masha fainted.

*

Now she was lying on a mattress in the former vegetable store behind the kitchens alongside the woman from the shot-up Zhiguli. Elina and a nurse from the hotel spent two hours on her, they staunched the bleeding and succeeded in extracting the bullet from the back of her neck, but Masha fainted again in the process. They couldn't tell if it had snagged her spinal cord, but it had burrowed in between her top two vertebrae. If only there were a hospital in the city where they could hitch her up to the right instruments.

The only thing that occurred to Igor was to take her diary and make a brief entry in it on her behalf. There was no other way he could help her. She was lying there, motionless, and refused to come round.

The entire basement had become airless, such air as there was was heavy and oily, and he was suffocating. He set off up the side stairs, as far as he could go. All the way to the debris on the fifth floor, where he'd never been before. The Hotel Europa had once had six floors, but the topmost no longer existed, and even here, on the fifth, he had to scramble over bits of ruined wall. He rounded the corner of the corridor and was lashed by an ice-cold wind. At the end of the corridor ahead of him the wall had gone completely; the red runner ran into a void.

He reached the very edge and looked out. In the city below him not a single light shone, the darkness broken only by blazing fires. Up in the sky the moon was skinny and crisp. He could sense the sea somewhere in the distance. To his left the chimneys and smelting furnaces of the iron and steel works reared up in dark silhouettes. There was fighting there now as well, the iron heart of Mariupol was on the brink of a heart attack. In the flashes of explosions he saw, perhaps for the first time in his life, no smoke belching from the chimneys. But there was smoke rising everywhere else and the air reeked of burning. A new blast of ice-cold wind lashed him across the face and at that very instant someone poked him in the back.

Just enough to give him a fright, but not to send him flying.

'Impressive sight, eh?' It was that girl again. 'I pop up here for a fag every night when I come off shift.'

She came and stood next to him and took a deep breath. Again she was wearing just that black nightie and the same make-up as usual: cat-lines about the eyes, red lips, and this time she'd got some perfume on.

'What would've 'appened if Masha'd made a wish that time?' he asked.

'Right at the beginning, that time by the aquarium? Of course, I'd have had to make it come true for her.'

''Cause you knew it were 'er last?'

'Oof, you're a bit down today. Come with me, I'll show you my room,' she said, turning, then she took a few almost dancing steps along the long red carpet. She was barefoot and the next gust of wind revealed to Igor that under her black nightie she'd got nothing else on. He set off after her like after a bitch who was just itching for it, though he was clear in his mind that the only thing really itching for anything was death.

This was his first time and it was like having sex with a bottomless pit. She strangled him with her long black hair, her blue nails dug into his temples. He opened his mouth and she spat in it, he touched her red lips and she bit him and drew blood. She sat astride him and he had to lick her anus, then she stood erect and peed on him from a height. That was the end of the foreplay, then came the real initiation, the raping and the ravishing.

Masha died that same night. When he woke up, the sexpot had gone. He went down to the ground floor and saw Elina, his mother and the rest, standing around the aquarium.

Light was descending on them through a hole in the ceiling and Elina was just reciting:

'I weep and I wail as I think upon death and see how the beauty of mankind created in the image of God lies here unlovely, deprived of its lustre and lacking all semblance. O, how unwonted is this?'

'O, how unwonted is this.' they mumbled after her.

'What mystery has befallen us? How have we succumbed to dissolution?'

'What mystery has befallen us. How have we succumbed to dissolution.'

He thrust his way through and saw Masha in the glass coffin that had been prepared for her from the start. Her snakelets crawled about her shoulders and in her little hands she was clutching her diary with the unicorn. The bottom of the aquarium was strewn with fine sea sand, its walls bedecked with the pale imprints of water weed as well as those lines and signatures left by the people from the hotel who'd marked the gradual drop in the water level until there was none left at all. He reached in his pocket and dribbled onto Masha's chest the small amount of sand that he'd put there when he'd still thought of it as a memento or to go into an hourglass. And he reminded himself what he'd promised on the last page of her diary: that thanks to Elina's iPhone he *would* catch up wi' that Cossack bastard sooner or later.

Swans

The car had been a birthday present. Yekaterina celebrated her fortieth three months ago and still hasn't got used to all the features that are different in a Tesla. In a Tesla, in the second half of her life, in the new situation in which we two find ourselves, at close quarters, *pas de deux*.

She wasn't that fussed about having a Tesla, which is why Ilya had to give it to her as a present. That was his way: overwhelming her with tokens of goodwill, bribing her with gifts. In the summer he'd wanted to drown her in the newly added pool, and when that failed he almost strangled her with a gold chain, and so now he'd set this Model Y on her. At least that's how I see it, from the worm's eye view of my own youth.

Would her white Tesla actually know how to apply its own brakes? I'm imagining Yekaterina's run up against some blockage riddled with red brake lights, hence she's not here yet. Suddenly it's not just the van in front, but all the vehicles in all the lanes around her. Any moment now a government convoy will come charging along Kutuzov Avenue, in all likelihood including the odd Merc with black-tinted windows and a Chechnya number plate beginning with 95. The avenue is so wide it's more like an airport runway, no traffic lights, and instead of crash barriers running down the middle it has a lane reserved for people from the FSB and Moscow city hall, for types managerial and magisterial, for Orthodox and unorthodox clergy, for members of the Duma, bigwigs, middlewigs and littlewigs. Woe betide those who haven't yet grasped that if one person wants to gallop past fast, all the rest have to hold their horses.

So Yekaterina is stuck there and I'm waiting for her here, waiting in the black swan costume hidden beneath my coat.

And Yekaterina is the white swan.

It's often cast as a twin role for one prima ballerina, but there are two of us.

Elon Musk thinks that a driver stuck in a traffic jam can pick a soap opera from her display screen or switch on some karaoke and croak along to it. But that's not for Yekaterina, all Yekaterina does is redo her lips in the mirror in the old-fashioned way, compress them and look back at herself briefly: so, this is me, not even bold make-up can conceal the wrinkles round my eyes, and as for that roll of fat above my cheekbone . . . She's fussing a bit too much, wouldn't you say? She recently remarked in the bathroom that it was high time she started to rejuvenate, Ilya would pay for any Botox, there'd be plenty left over for silicon as well, What d'you reckon? she'd said with a wink in my direction. I patted her on the bottom, 'Don't mention him at my place, don't mention him this evening', and I switched on the news. But that didn't improve matters because, as she put it, she'd spent her entire adult life with Putin.

True enough, if she'd been forty at the year's end, then Puss-puss Putin had first flushed the loo in the Kremlin less than a week after her eighteenth. And he must have flushed it because back then his bodyguards hadn't yet started collecting his poo. At least that's what they say: that these days they collect his turds lest they fall into enemy hands to reveal what shit is in them. Do they carry little bags with them like when someone's walking a slightly too rough-haired dachshund?

Never mind, that time on New Year's Eve 1-9-9-9, they broadcast two speeches on television: in the first, one paw was raised by an ailing, completely blotto Yeltsin, and in the other a totally fresh, lean Putin wished everyone a happy new year, goodness, no, a happy new century!

*

Down the central reservation zoomed five black limousines, also ballet of a kind. I'm sitting in my white Tesla in a horribly tight top and a tulle skirt that's eating into my thighs, and to the sounds of orchestrated power Rothbart's henchmen come hurtling past.

You know what power's like in Russia, everything ever so overdone in case someone doesn't spot it: the fastest cars, the costliest yachts, such young mistresses!

The blocked traffic slowly started to move. On Kutuzov Avenue the police check not speeds but the smoothness of the through-flow, no surprise, then, that Moscow's jeunesse dorée holds it as a point of honour to race along it, at least at night, at

200 kmph. Mimesis of power. And the fatal accident rate is there to match, one blackspot being right here, at the crossroads with the third Moscow ringroad. It's said that these are geopathogenic zones, or that bulldozers chewed up an old cemetery as the road was being built and the dead are now exacting revenge, but Occam's razor can get by without such twaddle: all those deaths are adequately explained by alcohol, eight cylinders and flooring the accelerator.

Anna must already be wondering where I am, she may even think I've given up on it. She acts like the one who's never in doubt, hence the secondary role has become mine. Or perhaps she never is in doubt, hence the cobalt hair.

The traffic was getting heavier, somewhere the air filter can be switched on, if only one could click one's way through to it, how *does* one click one's way to clean air?

It all began when she handed me that seminar paper with the title 'I'm a Russian Rocket'. So politics had been there between us from the outset, let's be clear about that. She'd been inspired by popular videos shot from the homing heads of guided missiles—from the privileged perspective of an optical direction finder she could describe the ground as it got nearer, a street, building, back yard and that family there in the yard, a family ringed with a circle, a family marked with a cross. Bang. At the end of the very first paragraph there was a mute explosion, a target annihilated. Then Anna sidestepped into history, a kind of *changement de pied*, she recalled the Gulf War, the first war to be broadcast live, and in no time she was arguing that Russia, with a twenty-five-year delay, tried the same tack in Syria. During the Gulf War, CNN came up with a proposal that some of the attacks could be made at night, so it looked better on the news. In the case of Syria, Anna wrote about 'the news porn on Channel 1'. That really could be extraordinarily detailed: it looked as if the optical tracking system could even detect the mood of a target as the explosion flung it against a wall and whether it had had a lamb kebab for dinner, or roasted-aubergine pasta.

What was I to do with a paper like that? It was well known that she would chant slogans on opposition marches and light candles on the Bolshoy Moskvoretsky Bridge by the little Boris Nemtsov memorial. At one demonstration she was even said to have sat down in front of a member of the OMON riot police and read out to him Article 31 of the constitution, which guarantees the right of peaceful assembly. And under interrogation she'd maintained that she'd only been revising for an exam in constitutional law, ha ha! It was hard not to admire her, but it wasn't surprising that even at school she'd been on parole. Officially for 'the promotion of non-traditional sexual relations', to use the wording in Jelena Mizulina's anti-gay law. The actual issue was that she'd showered the refectory with leaflets advertising a concert by the Night Snipers rock band, whose singer had recently left her husband for another girl member of the band. So it was obvious that if I blew the thing up Anna would be out of Lomonosov University, out of the Department of

Jurisprudence and Political Science, in double-quick time. I had her in my power.

I could have secured her removal, but instead I invited her for coffee in an out-of-the-way place far away from the university. Why? Because her work wasn't just good, it was brilliant—and I know what that's worth. But also to warn her. 'Russians feel cheated, but they only believe the television, and that is what's actually cheating them. Just as long as there isn't a war, as I repeat constantly, because if war does break out it will always have their approval, they are patriots after all,' she had written. I wanted to warn her, but truth to tell, in that coffee shop, she was the one who made an impression on me, not me on her. At one moment I registered how upright she sat, and I adjusted my own posture to match.

*

Yekaterina was almost twice my age, but when she undressed in my presence, it looked as if she was doing it for the first time in her life: her belly blushed. She was twice as old as me and her underwear cost ten times as much as mine, but it transpired that I'd slept with more people than she had: we had had the same number of boys, but then my girls, they were extra. She'd last been with someone other than Ilya before she'd even met Ilya, poor little faithful mite. But in fact I was impressed by her fidelity, unlike Ilya, who turned it to his account and who didn't impress me one bit.

You might say I'd got off with her, but that doesn't quite explain why I'm freezing here and now on the Kremlin

Embankment with a black swansdown clip in my hair and ballet shoes inside my felt boots. I might say that I'd tried it on with her and it worked, but to that you'd have to say what you reckon I'm trying on with you.

I didn't write the essay just as matter of course work, I wrote it explicitly for her. Yekaterina wasn't one of the lecturers, she was *the* lecturer. I wrote the essay over the course of one solid week, the first time I'd ever put so much effort into any course-work. I wanted to capture her attention, because she made herself the centre of attention all the time. When I was in the first year, she was one of very few academics to use the hashtag #ImNotAfraidToSay, our national variant of #MeToo. Then I heard all sorts about her: that she demands attention, that she makes herself out to be a poor little soul, that it's about fighting for her career, that she's not particularly attractive after all. I think that's all rubbish and the bench agrees, so back to the matter in hand: she hadn't been afraid to say she'd been harassed by the former dean. Not that she'd named him, but anyone wishing to could put two and two together. As always in such cases, half the academic community made five, but there was quite a to-do anyway. Both at the faculty, though the old monster had meanwhile gone off to a dacha somewhere, and, above all, at Yekaterina's.

She began about it herself, when she slept at mine for the third time. We were lying side by side on a folding settee and she asked if she could smoke. Now I don't smoke indoors, but something told me I should oblige her. I went to open the window and on the way back poked her in the belly button.

Just to be clear, every second woman in this country has been raped. And recently the Duma had to adopt a statute under which domestic violence isn't a crime, just so the courts could function normally! So it can definitely not be said that sexual harassment is taboo—sexual harassment is a national sport, an item set firmly in our national tradition and culture. At the closing ceremony of the Olympic Games in Sochi, Puss-puss Putin could easily have celebrated our supremacy in this international discipline as well; incidentally, that same morning he'd approved the invasion of Crimea, which shows just how sex-starved he must have been. So, Yekaterina couldn't understand why Ilya was so fussed that she'd pointed a finger at the dean. When all's said and done, he was her husband and should have smacked him in the chops himself, right? Except he wasn't that bothered that it had happened: what really got up his nose was that she'd used that hashtag. 'One time he came home in a particularly good mood and it all came tumbling out,' she told me. 'He was bothered that now all his mates would get turned on following what I'd described, that they'd all have visions of me with themselves in the role of the dean. I nearly choked: "Turned on, you say? They'll get turned on by the thought of the dean stubbing his cigarette out on me? And did it turn you on the first time I told you about it?" And do you know what he said? "Depends." Depends, he said. And then he went on, but I only heard the next bit from the other side of the door he'd just slammed: "But then, you are still quite a cracker!"'

I turned off the light, took Yekaterina by the hand and we went out onto the balcony, both in just our underwear. Just for a minute, while the cold was still refreshing. Down beneath us in the courtyard someone was parking their car, the red lights briefly seeping into the snow. We pressed ourselves against the wall in case the neighbour looked up.

The way I took it was that after years of marriage she was diffident and in a sense parched, and I was the forbidden fruit that she'd bitten into from a kind of despair. I was a rocket, but only short-range, everyone knew that of me. But on that balcony, in the middle of a February night, all that divided us was the different quantity of time that had flowed through our bodies: hers long and thin like when you stretch chewing gum, and mine, on which there's nothing to be said.

We got back into bed and I could think of nothing better to do than to start stroking her. And I made a thorough job of it, then, from her clammy belly, I asked: 'So, what shall we do?'

*

I first saw *Swan Lake* when I was three and a bit. I was standing in front of the television, touching the ballerinas with my fingertips until I got a nasty shock from the static. That must have been in March 1985 when General Secretary Chernenko died and Soviet TV didn't know what to do. Just like the year before, the time Andropov's kidneys gave out. And eighteen months before that, Brezhnev's big heart—back in those days there wasn't a lot to be said for the organs of general secretaries. Brezhnev could keep travelling abroad because he was running on batteries, but Andropov no longer travelled, needing to be constantly plugged into the mains.

In the mumbo-jumbo of our historiography, my early child-hood is called 'the quinquennium of glorious obsequies'. But the main thing I recall from any such political matters is *Swan Lake*. The television also put it on in August 1991 during the anti-Gorbachev putsch, but by then I'd long had my ballet shoes, tights and scrunchies and three times a week I'd meet up after school with my lookalikes in the hall of mirrors.

So my ballet history is a purely Soviet one. But it wasn't until Anna told me she'd put down ballet as part of her PE require-ment at university that I realized why she was also sitting bolt upright in that coffee house.

Ballet and law have something in common: discipline and precision. And that whether in ballet shoes or court shoes you'll still ruin your toes.

That evening, in the bedroom of her flat, we went and stood together in front of the mirror. It had been her grandmother's flat, her beads still hung from the mirror frame and on the wall to the left was a photo of her grandmother's father in uniform. Anna claimed he'd fought to defend Stalingrad, but couldn't fight back against Stalin, which could suggest all manner of things. Anyway, beneath his severe gaze we carefully rehearsed our *plié* and *demi-plié* and *relevé*. Ilya assumed I was at a depart-mental meeting, but for now I was standing behind Anna, adjusting her arm position and poking my nose into that cobalt hair. She'd dyed it only recently and it reeked of oxide.

At one moment she glanced at me in the mirror and said: 'We look alike. We look alike, but we've no need of any Prince Siegfried to get us mixed up. Do we?'

The war began two days later. I'd stayed at home that day, but Anna hadn't hesitated for one moment, without consulting me she'd produced a homemade placard and together with several thousand others she'd headed for Pushkin Square. OMON units were already waiting for them. People could still be arrested for failing to observe the anti-Covid measures, but laws could be updated quickly. Today a placard saying 'NO TO WAR!' can be prosecuted under the newly inserted paragraph 280.3 of the penal code as discrediting the Russian military. When the need arises our lawgivers can work very fast. After decades of obligatory Soviet pacifism, a call for peace had become a crime overnight. I noted that the police had even arrested a woman who'd come out onto the square carrying a blank placard. In short, Russia had reached a magical period in its history: everyone knew what had been written on it in invisible writing, those intrepid warriors in their black helmets could read it just as well as the woman who'd not written it there with such finesse. And out of the dark holes of the collective subconscious came crawling the grossest spectres and began debating on Channel 1 . . .

Anna was lucky to have been charged with nothing worse than endangering public health. She wound up in a police van, spent the night at a police station and came home the next day. And I was waiting for her.

*

Is Yekaterina parked up somewhere? Perhaps at one of those charging points that have sprung up all over Moscow? I can just imagine her alighting from her Tesla in her white swan tights and, abracadabra, there's a police patrol car. They find it a bit weird as Yekaterina, with all the charm of a university lecturer, explains that she's filming a commercial. The Tesla is floating on the roadway as silently as a swan on a lake, and is just as elegant, which is why the director had dreamed up a shoot with the Tesla and a ballerina where they would dance together in front of St Basil's Cathedral. Of course, it's aimed only at the Russian market, no worries, Nikita Mikhalkov knows what he's doing.

When Yekaterina came up with the idea that we could do a ballet number on Red Square itself, I gasped. At the time, walls had been sprayed with images of ballerinas, those four in a row, the glorious *pas de quatre* from *Swan Lake*; anyone who wanted to understand did understand, just as they understood the eight crosses or the inscription 'Cargo 200', those coded messages attached to bodies being repatriated from the battlefront. But to put on one's pointe shoes and head straight for Red Square, that amounted to assisted suicide—and the militia were sure to do the assisting.

'We can't say nothing, can we?' she said. Yet we can't *say* anything at all. We shall protest with the aid of that which is most Russian, most tragic and most pointless. On my PC I had a programme capable of assigning me a foreign IP address. Thanks to that I saw, the same day, shots taken in Bucha. I stared at them over and over again, totally hypnotized. *That* was the most Russian, most tragic and most pointless.

And that was what tipped the scale.

The same evening, we watched the *Pas de quatre* on YouTube. We joined hands and tried it out in front of the mirror, at least the two of us. And all those perfectly synchronized, tiny steps, the leg-crossing and dazzling footwork, as if the dancers had a shared nervous system, as if they had a single soul split into four . . . We couldn't manage any of it. I'd once heard that the ballerinas in one company even coordinated their periods, so interlocked were they, but that definitely didn't apply to us. We may have been two swans, but while Yekaterina really did have a long white neck, I mostly employed my big orange beak.

'Do you remember what you said the first time we stood here together?' she asked. We were sitting on the floor opposite each other, munching pineapple slices and thinking what to do next. 'You said we looked alike but had no need of any Prince Siegfried to get us mixed up. This is good,' she went on and stuck a forkful of the pale-yellow fruit in my mouth. 'In *Swan Lake* the white swan and the black swan never appear on stage together, except when taking their final bow. It's either–or, and the basis of this disjunctive relationship is Prince Siegfried. He's the one who makes choices, he's the one they all adulate, he's the one who makes all the decisions, even if they're always the wrong ones.'

'I love you,' I let slip.

She let out a whistle. 'Maybe the time's come for the white and black swans to dance only ever together. What's *Swan Lake* about? It's about a girl turned by magic into a swan who can only be liberated by love. But her prince gets chatted up by another and she pines to death. It's brilliant. Perhaps we're all enchanted white swans, though rather than that bad egg Siegfried we need to discover our own black swan.'

For the next three weeks we practised every day. During the day we acted with restraint, each leaving the house separately, and me never joining her in the car. We indulged in only one dodgy activity: buying second-hand mirrors and hauling them upstairs. We lined the bedroom with them and tried to polish our choreography, that's to say what was left of Fokin after we'd divided him up according to our aptitudes, that's to say our ineptitudes.

And as a bonus we sank our teeth into each other in that mirror-filled bedroom. Yekaterina lost her coyness and performed wild bedroom *échapés* and *développés* as if political protest had also liberated her sexually. She was fed up of Putin, fed up of Ilya, fed up of her own life. Like all people, she longed for freedom, orgasm and death and I was grateful to her for being able to provide at least one of those. To want to achieve more struck me as presumptuous in the circumstances.

*

All it required was to drive through Novyi Arbat and park the Tesla in the underground carpark beneath Zaryadye Park, which had been created some years previously to replace the gigantic Hotel Rossiya. The Kremlin was nearby, and it goes without saying that there were more cameras than birds in the trees. The agreement was that Anna and I would meet at the end of

Varvarka Street five minutes after the chimes, then, warmly wrapped in our overcoats, we'd make straight for Red Square.

'Somewhere in a human heart lies Red Square,' she had written in lipstick on a mirror a few days before, before she went to bed. I found it next morning while she was still asleep and as I brushed my teeth and with white froth around my mouth I played a game of spot the meaning:

Somewhere in the human heart is a place that slopes downwards in both directions.

Somewhere in the human heart is a place where there's room for everything, but where everything also gets lost.

Somewhere in the human heart is a place where the smell of Stalin's favourite Herzegovina Flor tobacco still drifts through the air.

Somewhere in the human heart is a place where the world is at its roundest, as Osip Mandelshtam wrote of Red Square.

But maybe Anna meant that somewhere in the human heart is the place where the monastery of the Miracle of the Archangel Michael, destroyed by the Bolsheviks, still stands.

Tchaikovsky knew that for *Swan Lake* to be really sensational it had to end in tragedy. The forsaken white swan hurls herself into the storm-torn waters of a lake, followed by the distraught Siegfried as soon as he awakes to his fateful error. But that kind of ending didn't suit the constructors of Soviet optimism and so they cast a different one: Prince Siegfried overcomes the sorcerer Rothbart and lives happily with Odette to the end of his days. But that was to open a Pandora's box and

Swan Lake today has dozens of different endings. New York City Ballet, the Royal Ballet in London, the Paris Opera Ballet, the Royal Danish Ballet, the Russian State Ballet of Siberia— they all have their own ending, each one worse than the next.

The beautiful, tired story traverses the world, looking for ways to turn out.

That's what I'm thinking about as I take the lift from the underground carpark up and out onto the cold surface of Moscow. Of course, *Swan Lake* premiered right here, at the Bolshoi Theatre, fifteen minutes away. Of course, I myself first saw it live here a century or so later.

Anna is standing by the terrace wall that surrounds St Basil's Cathedral and smoking. Having spotted me, she stubs her cigarette out, tosses the butt down a drain and sets off towards me.

The girl's looking like a cross between a ballerina and a female punk. She's made up her eyes in black, from the bridge of her nose to her temples, where the lines are frayed like feathers. Her lips are deep red, she's plastered her cobalt-blue hair onto her scalp with setting lotion and set a swansdown clip in it. From her long coat her calves peek out in translucent black nylons, and a shiny decorative ribbon is poking out from her high felt boots. Everything has been contrived so that we can simply remove our coats, kick our boots off and launch into our swan song.

Neither of us has any future now. Nothing offers any greater relief from pain. Viewed from the future, the present is but a past that's long been over and done with, but you only see that by the time you have no future.

None: wasting no more time, we set off along by the terrace wall surrounding the church, passing the monument to Minin and Pozharsky, with the parting of Red Square's thighs before us. To the right the czars' tribune, to the left the long phallic shadow of the Spassky Tower, ahead the Lenin Mausoleum. We glance at each other, kiss each other, that's the way it is—politics had been there between us since the beginning and will be with us to the end. We take our wireless earbuds from our pockets and fix them in place, each of us doing the other's like an exchange of wedding rings.

This will be our *silent disco.* Tchaikovsky will be playing from my phone for Anna and from hers for me. So if one of us ends up too far from the other, we'll know it's all over: we can only separate to within the range of our Bluetooth. We're bonded via our blue teeth.

I'm in no doubt that the cameras of the Kremlin will be recording our *pas de deux* from every angle. They'll be recording a black swan and a white swan, Odette and Odile, a former future reader in the Department of Jurisprudence and Political Science of the Law Faculty of the Lomonosov University and her former future PhD student, dancing as if their lives depend on it against the backdrop of Red Square. How long will it take for someone in front of the bank of monitors in the control room to realize what it is they're watching? How long before they realize that this dance is presaging the same old thing?

Author's Note

One has to disavow one's own truths in order to discover something new. I've been telling myself for so long that literature calls for hindsight that in the course of four months—from the beginning of March to the end of June 2022—I wrote a book that, with no hindsight, draws on what was actually happening during the first phase of the war in Ukraine. Some of the stories, most notably 'Aquarium', came about almost as a live transmission—I would follow the news to discover how my story was going to end.

In reality no book is exclusively the work of its author. I am grateful to Tereza Matějčková for reading each story the minute it was written and talking with me about what it was I needed to be saying. Miroslav Balaštík added his editoral comments to the stories and encouraged me to keep on writing. And Olga Trávníčková saw to it that such peppily emerging texts—I'd be onto the next without having gone back through the one before—kept some sort of linguistic unity.

A portion of the book came into being during a residency I was granted on the 'Mikulov Reads' programme. My thanks are due to Petr Šesták not only for inviting me to Mikulov, but also for opening various doors there for me, so that now I know who lives behind them. A month later, I completed the manuscript in Tábor. I have dedicated the book to Oksana, my Tábor friend whose roots are Ukrainian, but I also had a great time there thanks to Lenka, Majda, Jana, Eva, Zita, Honza and Kryštof. I never saw Bára, but she'd lent me her flat for a month—thanks Bára!

Jednota Co-op, Tábor
8 July 2022